PRAISE FC

"The Seduction of Lord Stone is romantic, emotional, sexy and funny. In fact, everything I have come to expect from Anna Campbell. I'm looking forward to reading the other Dashing Widows' stories." —*RakesandRascals.com*

"With her marvelous combination of humor and poignancy Anna Campbell writes in such a way that every story of hers has a special meaning and remains like a sentimental keepsake with those fortunate enough to read her work!" —*JeneratedReviews.com*

"Lord Garson's Bride is a well written and passionate story that touched my heart and sent my emotions on a rollercoaster ride. I particularly recommend this book for fans of convenient marriages, and those who enjoy seeing a deserving character find out that love is lovelier the second time around." —*Roses Are Blue Reviews*

"Campbell immediately hooks readers, then deftly reels them in with a spellbinding love story fueled by an addictive mixture of sharp wit, lush sensuality, and a wealth of well-delineated characters."—*Booklist, starred review, on A Scoundrel by Moonlight*

"With its superbly nuanced characters, impeccably crafted historical setting, and graceful writing shot through with scintillating wit, Campbell's latest lusciously sensual, flawlessly written historical Regency ... will have romance readers sighing happily with satisfaction."—*Booklist, Starred Review, on What a Duke Dares*

"Campbell makes the Regency period pop in the appealing third Sons of Sin novel. Romantic fireworks, the constraints of custom, and witty banter are combined in this sweet and successful story."—*Publishers Weekly on What a Duke Dares*

"Campbell is exceptionally talented, especially with plots that challenge the reader, and emotions and characters that are complex and memorable."—*Sarah Wendell, Smart Bitches Trashy Books, on A Rake's Midnight Kiss*

"A lovely, lovely book that will touch your heart and remind you why you read romance."—*Liz Carlyle, New York Times bestselling author on What a Duke Dares*

"Campbell holds readers captive with her highly intense, emotional, sizzling and dark romances. She instinctually knows how to play on her readers' fantasies to create a romantic, deep-sigh tale."—*RT Book Reviews, Top Pick, on Captive of Sin*

"She's the mistress of dark, sexy and brooding and takes us into the dens of iniquity with humor and class."—*Bookseller-Publisher Australia*

"Anna Campbell is a master at drawing a reader in from the very first page and keeping them captivated the whole book through. Ms. Campbell's books are all on my keeper shelf and *Midnight's Wild Passion* will join them proudly. *Midnight's Wild Passion* is a smoothly sensual delight that was a joy to read and I cannot wait to revisit Antonia and Nicholas's romance again."—*Joyfully Reviewed*

"Ms. Campbell gives us...the steamy sex scenes, a heroine whose backbone is pure steel and a stupendous tale of lust and love and you too cannot help but fall in love with this tantalizing novel."—*Coffee Time Romance*

"Anna Campbell offers us again, a lush, intimate, seductive read. I am in awe of the way she keeps the focus tight on the hero and heroine, almost achingly so. Nothing else really exists in this world, but the two main characters. Intimate, sensual story with a hero that will take your breath away."—*Historical Romance Books & More*

ALSO BY ANNA CAMPBELL

Claiming the Courtesan

Untouched

Tempt the Devil

Captive of Sin

My Reckless Surrender

Midnight's Wild Passion

The Sons of Sin series:

Seven Nights in a Rogue's Bed

Days of Rakes and Roses

A Rake's Midnight Kiss

What a Duke Dares

A Scoundrel by Moonlight

Three Proposals and a Scandal

The Dashing Widows:

The Seduction of Lord Stone

Tempting Mr. Townsend

Winning Lord West

Pursuing Lord Pascal

Charming Sir Charles

Catching Captain Nash

Lord Garson's Bride

The Lairds Most Likely:

The Laird's Willful Lass

The Laird's Christmas Kiss

The Highlander's Lost Lady

Christmas Stories:

The Winter Wife

Her Christmas Earl

A Pirate for Christmas

Mistletoe and the Major

A Match Made in Mistletoe

The Christmas Stranger

Other Books:

These Haunted Hearts

Stranded with the Scottish Earl

CHARMING SIR CHARLES

THE DASHING WIDOWS BOOK 5

ANNA CAMPBELL

Serenade Publishing

ISBN: 978-0-6483987-7-6

Cover design: By Hang Le

Print editions published by Serenade Publishing
www.serenadepublishing.com

To my dear friend Annie West.

CHAPTER ONE

Hanover Square, London, May 1829

*W*hen London's handsomest man married a lovely Dashing Widow, half the world turned out to witness the event.

Sally Cowan, Countess of Norwood, stared in astonishment at the surging crowds around St. George's. She cast a doubtful glance across the open barouche to where Amy Mowbray, today's bride, sat, resplendent in heavy silk the color of new butter. "Oh, dear, I hope the carriage gets through the crush."

"Of course it will." Amy smiled back with the poise that was new since she'd fallen in love with Lord Pascal. "Nothing's going to spoil today."

It turned out Amy was right. The crowds gave a

loud and sustained cheer as the bride and her attendants arrived. The mass of people parted to form a clear path toward the row of pillars across the church's entrance. They cheered again when Sally, Amy's sister Helena, and her sister-in-law Morwenna stepped down, and more enthusiastically still when Amy stood before them in her full glory.

Despite her miserable experience as a wife, Sally loved weddings. Especially big, extravagant ones where the bride and groom were deliriously in love. They reminded her that not all men were ignorant swine like the late Lord Norwood, and that not every marriage was a grim ordeal like hers had been.

She had no interest in taking another husband, but she very much approved of her friends finding their perfect matches. And today's wedding was undoubtedly a perfect match. She'd been looking forward to this ever since the start of the season, when Amy caught the dashing Lord Pascal's eye.

"Pascal will be dazzled," Sally said. "Amy, you're a vision."

"Thank you," Amy said. "You know, I have you to thank for today. If you hadn't convinced me to come to London and kick up my heels, I'd still be whispering sweet nothings to my Herefords."

"Instead of to your besotted bridegroom," Sally said in a teasing tone. "Believe me, I take full credit for how events turned out."

"You do look lovely, Amy." Morwenna's dark blue eyes glittered with unshed tears.

Sally caught Morwenna's hand and pressed it in silent comfort. Inevitably this must bring back memories of her own wedding to Captain Robert Nash, a union which ended tragically when Robert drowned off the coast of South America.

"No tears, Morwenna," Helena, Lady West, said, although her eyes were suspiciously bright. "Otherwise Amy will run off and find some cattle to talk to, instead of staying here and getting married."

Amy, famous for her farming expertise, stood uncharacteristically docile, while Sally twitched at her skirts to straighten them. "You know, the dairy cows in St. James's Park aren't far away."

"Amy…" Sally said in warning.

"Don't worry, Sally and Hel." Amy gave a gurgle of happy laughter. "I'm not going anywhere. Not even the discovery of a new disease in beef cattle could lure me away from Pascal today."

"I'm glad to hear it." Silas Nash, Lord Stone, strode up to them and kissed his youngest sister's cheek. "Good morning, Helena, Morwenna, and Sally. You look beautiful, Amy."

Amy smiled at Silas, and Sally again noticed the strong resemblance between brother and sister. Both tall and tawny and striking, in contrast to Helena's flashing dark good looks.

"Thank you. You've scrubbed up pretty well yourself." Amy sniffed ostentatiously and gave Silas a smile. "Not a hint of compost, I'm delighted to note."

Silas, a renowned botanist, laughed without resentment. "Caro checked before she let me out." As ever when he mentioned his beloved wife, his expression warmed. "And she banned me from entering my greenhouse this morning."

"Bravo, Caroline," Sally said drily.

She stifled a pang of envy when she saw how joy had transfigured the usually prosaic Amy. Sally had never been in love, and couldn't imagine she ever would be, now she reached the advanced age of thirty-one.

At seventeen, her parents had pushed her into marrying a man she'd quietly grown to despise, although she'd always presented a brave face to the world. Norwood's death in a riding accident four years ago had released her to a widowhood that she'd thoroughly enjoyed. And intended to enjoy even more.

But observing Amy today, Sally couldn't help recognizing that freedom wasn't the only thing a woman could hope for in this life.

Unsuitable thoughts, when she should be devoting her attention to her friend's nuptials.

Silas extended his arm to Amy. "Ready?"

"Eager." She slid her gloved hand into the crook of his elbow.

"Well, you have done this before," Helena said slyly.

Amy's smile was beatific. "No, I haven't."

Even cynical Helena wasn't proof against Amy's happiness, and her voice softened. "No, indeed you haven't."

Her heart brimming with elation for Amy and regret that such a transformative love had forever passed her by, Sally firmed her hold on her bouquet of violets and lily-of-the-valley. She took her place in front of Silas and Amy. Helena and Morwenna lined up behind the bride. A flourish of music from inside the church, and they moved forward.

The church was crowded, too. Sally glanced around the elegant congregation and saw so many people who had become important to her over recent years. Lord and Lady Kenwick and their family. Caroline, Lady Stone, who had banned her husband from his horticultural experiments this morning. Sally's dear niece Meg, her protegée this season. A few pews back, Meg's handsome suitor, Sir Charles Kinglake.

Sir Charles looked breathtaking in a black coat that emphasized his broad shoulders and impressive chest. Admiration made Sally's heart skip a beat. What a fine figure of a man Meg had caught for herself—if the chit could just bring the elegant baronet to the point of proposing.

When he noticed Sally looking at him, he sent her an approving smile. A dimple appeared in his lean cheek, and laughter lines deepened around his dark eyes.

She so appreciated how he always acknowledged

her as a person in her own right. After all, as Meg's widowed aunt and chaperone, most men would consider her an inconvenience. Gratitude for his exquisite manners made her silly heart perform another leap. Even for a woman past the giddy age, it was a thrill to have all that masculine appeal focused on her.

Sir Charles was all that a girl could wish in a husband. Kind, sophisticated, rich. And madly attractive as well. Rich brown hair the color of strong coffee. Deep brown eyes. Tall and strong and vigorous. And an exceptionally nice smile.

Sally found herself smiling back at him as she walked up the aisle in front of Amy.

Meg was such a lucky girl.

Perhaps once Meg was safely married, Sally would revive her plan to extend her experience beyond her husband's inept fumblings. She might be too old to make a love match, but she wasn't too old to enjoy an amorous adventure or two, by heaven.

Norwood had been hopeless in bed, on the rare occasions when he joined her there at all. Whereas something about Sir Charles's air of effortless self-assurance hinted that he knew just what to do when he had a woman in his arms.

Today's wedding confirmed her decision. Why should Amy have all the fun? Soon, she'd choose a lover who was just like Sir Charles. A good man, but not so good that he didn't know how to pleasure her. It was time she discovered just what put that spark in Amy's hazel eyes when she looked at her bridegroom.

Sally ought to be blushing. These profane thoughts weren't appropriate in a church.

At the altar, she stepped aside and watched Amy present her hand to Gervaise Dacre, Lord Pascal, who today definitely lived up to his reputation as London's handsomest man. His golden good looks were extraordinary, nor could anyone mistake the glow of adoration in his deep blue eyes when he looked at his bride.

Amy was a lucky girl, too.

Well, once she'd married Meg off to Sir Charles, Sally intended to be another lucky girl. The only man who had shared her bed was unworthy of the honor. The next man she chose would show her just what she'd been missing all these years.

CHAPTER TWO

*S*ilas and Caroline hosted the wedding breakfast at their opulent house in Half Moon Street.

Sally paused for a moment near the ballroom's French doors, open onto the lush spring garden. Even London's capricious spring weather blessed today's festivities. Around her, conversation buzzed, spiked with joyous laughter, making it difficult to hear the string quartet Silas had hired for the occasion.

"The ranks of the Dashing Widows are thinning," Sir Charles said, coming up beside her and passing her a glass of champagne.

Sally turned from studying the jubilant newlyweds to bestow a wide smile on the tall man in perfectly tailored formal black. The day's romantic atmosphere must be affecting even her prosaic soul. At the sight of him, her heart performed that odd little wobble again.

"Someone told you about our pact, did they?"

"I went out celebrating with Pascal, Kenwick and West last night." He regarded his full glass with a lack enthusiasm that amused her. "In their cups, they gave me the story behind the nickname."

She, Morwenna, and Amy had made a pact to have some fun in society and set aside old, unhappy memories. They'd taken as their example the first three Dashing Widows, Caroline, now Lady Stone, Fenella, now Lady Kenwick, and Helena. Eight years ago, all three women had put off their mourning and gone out to find love and new, fulfilled lives.

"I won't mind at all if I'm the last Dashing Widow standing." His easy manner settled her unsteady pulse and reminded her how remarkably comfortable she'd always felt with him. "I'd be delighted to see Morwenna find happiness, too."

Sympathy turned his brown eyes velvety. "How long is it since her husband was lost at sea?"

"Nearly five years. At first, I wasn't sure bringing her to London was a good idea, but lately she seems to be finding her feet and enjoying herself."

Sir Charles took a sip of his champagne and tilted his eyebrows to where Morwenna stood talking to a dark-haired man in a blue coat. "Garson seems to be enjoying her."

"I don't think…" Sally said in shock.

Then she closed her mouth and studied her lovely black-haired friend, striking in a lavender gown that turned her blue eyes purple. Eyes that were once dull with sorrow, but which now sparkled as she laughed up at the tall man, looming over her with a rapt expression on his face.

"How on earth did you notice that and I didn't?" She and Morwenna—and Amy until today—shared a house this season, but they didn't live in each other's pockets. Nonetheless if Morwenna had accepted Garson's advances, surely Sally would have guessed.

Sir Charles shrugged, reminding her again of the imposing width of his shoulders. "You've been too busy chaperoning Meg to take note of your friends' romances."

Sally cast a fond glance to her pretty niece, who was deep in conversation with Vernon Grange, Lord West. If she knew Meg—and of course, she did—they were discussing equine bloodlines. West bred champion racehorses, and Meg had been horse mad since before she could walk. "Luckily she's not much trouble."

She returned her attention to Morwenna, who was no longer the wan, grief-stricken waif of a few months ago. Was it possible she'd taken Lord Garson as a lover? He was a good few years older than she was, but he was an attractive man. Anyway, Sir Charles was nearly ten years older than Meg, and Sally was in favor of that match.

"You know, I don't think they've gone that far," Sir Charles murmured in her ear. "Garson has his sights on Morwenna, but I believe he's seeking a wife rather than a mistress."

Sally flinched at how easily he'd guessed what she was thinking. She shot him a disapproving glance. "If you were any sharper, you'd cut yourself."

He laughed. He had a nice laugh. He had a nice voice, low and deep. She couldn't think of a better husband for Meg. His natural warmth boded well for a contented married life.

"So now Garson is pursuing Morwenna, I'd say the days of the Dashing Widows are definitely numbered."

Sally tried her champagne, enjoying the crisp flavor with its hint of dryness. A little like Sir Charles's conversation, in fact.

From the first, she'd liked talking to him. He was a sensible, intelligent man, qualities Meg mightn't appreciate fully at this stage. But Sally, having lived with a man neither sensible nor clever, knew that in the long term, her niece would come to value Sir Charles's good sense. "I'll have to gather some more Dashing Widows together, so I can keep the tradition going."

"Why on earth should you?" He settled that autumnal gaze on her, and his tone was thoughtful. "After all, you'll be married again yourself."

Sally jerked, and spilled a few drops of her champagne, luckily on the floor, not on her lovely bronze silk dress. She struggled to keep her voice from betraying how his words had sent a cold chill down her spine. "Oh, I'm well past marrying age."

"Utter nonsense," he said, with more emphasis than she thought her statement deserved.

Sally shook her head and smiled. "Oh, perhaps some old codger might take me on, to make his life comfortable and run his house. But where would be the fun in that?"

"There wouldn't be any." Sir Charles frowned at her. "You speak as if you're pushing fifty. When anyone with eyes can see you're an attractive woman in the prime of life."

"Why, thank you, sir," she said with an exaggerated flutter of her eyelashes. "You flatter me."

He didn't smile back. Which was odd. His sense of humor was another of the many things she admired about him. "Sally, I'm serious."

Startled, she stared at him, while disquiet stirred in her stomach.

Sally? Surely they weren't on terms where he should use her Christian name. She bit back a protest. If he was to marry Meg, she supposed she couldn't insist on the letter of propriety.

Had he been standing quite so close before? She'd never been so conscious of his height and power. The urge to deliver another frivolous answer withered under the unusually somber expression in his dark eyes.

"I'm too old for romance, Sir Charles." She placed a slight weight on his title. "And I have no other reason to marry. I'm well provided for. I have a lovely home. I have wonderful friends."

"What about companionship?" Her assertions left him visibly unimpressed. "Specifically of the masculine variety."

Her lips tightened. "A lover, you mean?"

He gestured with his champagne glass. "If you like."

Good God. What an extraordinary conversation.

In the two months he'd been in London, she and Sir Charles had never ventured into such murky waters. If they'd discussed love, it was always in connection to mythical beings in a painting. Venus and Mars. Cupid and Psyche. Diana and Actaeon. A thousand cupids flitting across canvases heaving with carousing gods and goddesses. Sir Charles was a famous art collector.

She shifted uncomfortably from one foot to the other and wished to heaven that Helena or Caro would come and rescue her from this odd conversation. But they were both on the other side of the room, curse them. "You put me to the blush, sir."

The tilt of Sir Charles's eyebrow hinted that he heard the off-kilter note in her answer, and his smile held an unfamiliar grimness. "You're too old to blush, Lady Norwood, if I paid one ounce of credence to this drivel you're spouting."

"Well, really," she began hotly, smarting at his sardonic tone, but stopped before she said something unforgiveable. To her relief, Meg was heading in their direction.

"Aunt Sally, Brandon wants to show off his new bays. Can I go driving with him this afternoon?"

To Sally's surprise, Sir Charles didn't seem altogether pleased that Meg interrupted their increasingly awkward discussion. Unless as was more likely, his pique had nothing to do with Sally, and everything to do with Meg seeking another man's company.

Blast him. If Sir Charles wanted a say over where Meg spent her time, he could damn well propose. He'd been dangling after the girl since he'd come to Town. Perhaps a little competition might bring him up to scratch.

He took a step back, and Sally sucked in a relieved breath. The intensity between them threatened to spoil the pleasant companionship she had come to rely upon.

When Sally was too distracted to answer immediately, Meg sent her a pleading look. "Please, Aunt. He's just bought them from Tattersalls, and he says they're magnificent steppers."

"Of course you may," Sally said, struggling to shake off her reaction to Sir Charles's manner. And her own odd reaction to him.

She passed her half-full glass to a footman. That bizarre conversation about marriage had quite spoiled her taste for champagne.

"Thank you, Aunt." Meg curtsied to Sir Charles. "It was a lovely wedding, wasn't it, Sir Charles?"

"Delightful." As he bowed, his expression softened

with the mixture of amusement and fondness that encouraged Sally to hope a wedding lay ahead. And reminded her that this prickle she felt in his presence meant nothing in the larger scheme.

What mattered was that he liked Meg and would make her a wonderful husband. Still, she had to struggle to shift her mind from their disconcerting exchange to the progress of his courtship.

Love was definitely in the air today. Even a complete novice to the emotion like her felt it. Would Amy and Pascal's nuptials inspire him to propose to Meg?

Sally couldn't believe he was toying with her niece. That would be both cruel and unprincipled, and she was convinced Sir Charles was neither.

Clearly eager to finalize arrangements for the outing, Meg returned to Brandon Deerham and his best friend and foster brother, Carey Townsend.

"Meg and Brand are just friends. There's nothing serious in it," Sally found herself saying, despite her earlier impulse to let him stew, not to mention the opportunity Meg's interruption offered to seek less demanding company.

"Of course there isn't." Sir Charles seemed surprised she'd felt the need to make the remark. "They're both so young. Sir Brandon must only be twenty or so."

Had Sally mistaken his resentment of Brand? Sir

Charles mustn't be the jealous type. Something else that forecast future happiness for his wife.

Her niece was bright and high-spirited, and a possessive husband might crush that vitality. Sally had bitter experience of a man who set out to turn a vivacious girl into a meek helpmeet.

"Too young for a gentleman to make a commitment, but not for a woman. I was married at seventeen."

"It's still too young."

Was that why he delayed his proposal? If so, he was taking a risk. He wasn't the only man in London to notice that her niece was pretty and good company. "Meg is eighteen, and much more levelheaded than I was at that age. I think an older man would steady her."

An older man like you, she wanted to say.

Devil take him, it was time he stated his intentions. This was really too bad of him. If he wasn't interested in marrying Meg this season, he should jolly well step aside and let some other eligible suitor step up.

"You're looking very fierce," he said, leaning closer with a welcome trace of his bantering manner. But she still couldn't relax in his company.

They'd been talking alone too long for strict decorum, but at a gathering like this, nobody would mind. Still, Sally suddenly felt as if he cut her off from the crowd, the way a sheepdog edged out a particular ewe from the herd.

Before today, she hadn't realized quite how tall he

was. But right now, she felt like a mighty oak overshadowed her. She raised puzzled eyes to his face, taking in the chiseled features. The square-cut jaw and long, straight nose. The watchful eyes under thick dark brows.

Her heart took another unsteady dive. He looked like he was on the verge of saying something important.

What on earth was happening? Was he about to ask her permission to pay his addresses to Meg?

"Sally…"

"Sally," she heard a voice say like an echo. "Amy is going upstairs to get ready to leave. Do you want to come and help her?"

At Helena's interruption, exasperation flashed in Sir Charles's dark eyes. For a fraught moment, Sally continued to stare into his face. Somewhere deep inside her, she wondered if she knew him at all. Today he wasn't the amusing, informative companion whose presence had so enriched these last weeks.

She gave herself a mental shake. Of course she knew him. He was her good friend and the perfect match for Meg. Weddings often had a strange effect on people—and unless she'd completely lost her mind, she was sure Sir Charles was contemplating a wedding of his own.

"Of course," she murmured, stepping past him toward Helena. She took her first full breath in what felt like hours. The chat had become rather oppressive, as if world-shaking revelations hovered close. "Will you excuse me, Sir Charles?"

He bowed. "I'll see you tomorrow night at the opera."

She smiled, surprised at the effort it took. "Meg and I look forward to it."

Which was a lie. Meg found the opera a complete bore, although she enjoyed meeting her friends in the interval.

"I'm glad to hear it."

"You two looked very chummy," Helena murmured, as they made their way up to the rooms Silas had set aside for his sister's use today.

Sally tried for a lighthearted tone, but her voice emerged unnaturally high. "I thought he was about to declare himself."

Helena stumbled to a stop on the stairs and stared at Sally with bright black eyes. "Sally, really?"

Sally gave her friend a puzzled glance. "He's been hanging after Meg for weeks. A proposal is well overdue."

The light ebbed from Helena's eyes, and she spoke in a flat voice. "Meg."

Sally frowned. Everyone was acting peculiar today. First Sir Charles calling her Sally when they were mere acquaintances, then that strange, fractious conversation about things he really had no right to comment upon. Now Helena acted as if she doubted Sally's sanity.

"Of course Meg," she said curtly. "The man must have come to Town in search of a wife. He's reached the age where he needs to set up his nursery. And Meg is perfect for him. He clearly agrees. In the last eight weeks, she's hardly appeared at an event without him paying his attentions."

"To Meg."

Sally made a sound of annoyance. "Plague take you, I can't see why you object. I thought you liked him."

Helena's laugh contained its usual sardonic edge. "Oh, I do. And I know you do, too."

"Of course I do. Otherwise I wouldn't want him to marry my niece. What in heaven's name is wrong with you?"

Helena's expression was disgusted. "There's nothing wrong with *me*."

And on that enigmatic note, she sailed into Amy's boudoir and left Sally scowling after her in complete bewilderment.

CHAPTER THREE

*S*ir Charles Kinglake was a fellow who appreciated the finer things in life. So usually a performance of "The Marriage of Figaro," featuring a famous Italian soprano, would have him alert to every note.

Instead he was too busy gnashing his teeth over the marriage of Charles Kinglake to give a fig for anyone else's nuptials, even Figaro's. He didn't pay Signora Strozzi's talents the attention they deserved.

He sat between Sally Cowan and her niece in his box at the Italian Opera House. Just behind him sat his other guests, the charming Lady Kenwick and her rough diamond, but brilliant husband. Sublime music flowed around him, but it might as well be tomcats yowling.

Charles felt rather like a frustrated tomcat himself. For the past two months, he'd existed in a lather of balked desire for a woman who persisted in thinking of him as a friend not a lover.

Right now, Sally's gloved hand draped over the edge of the box, mere inches from his. His hand curled against the chair arm as he fought the urge to reach out and touch her. She sat close enough for him to catch the enticing drift of her subtle perfume, flowers and lovely woman.

Yet for all the attention she paid to him as a potential husband, she might as well be in far Cathay. He bit back a growl. What the devil was wrong with Sally Cowan?

Sadly the answer to that question, on most levels, was not a thing.

She was absolutely delightful. Clever. Funny. Vivid. Stylish. Good-hearted.

He could fill a deuced three-volume novel with praise of her qualities.

Her expressive face with its bright green eyes and pointed chin might fall short of classical standards of beauty. Her long, thin nose might be a little off-center. Her mouth might be a tad wide to fit her features, although it provided a pleasing hint of a passionate nature. A passionate nature he desperately hoped to discover before he reached his old age.

But he found the quirks in her appearance more appealing than mere prettiness could ever be.

And nobody could criticize her figure. Long and graceful and lissome. He spent feverish nights dreaming of what she looked like naked. He'd wager her legs were a work of art to rival anything in his famed collection of old masters.

Not, by God, that he knew.

Apart from a dance, or taking her hand to help her into or out of a carriage, he hadn't touched her. Damn and blast it.

He'd known the minute he saw her across a crowded ballroom that she was the one for him. Nothing in his previous discreet liaisons had prepared him for this ferocious desire.

But even in the grip of this compulsion to have the lovely widow whatever it cost, he remained a percep- tive man. He'd swiftly realized that beneath Sally's air of confidence and good cheer, she was vulnerable. A pursuit too ardent was likely to frighten her away rather than win her.

So much against his masculine impulses, he reined in his immediate urge to claim and conquer. Instead of sweeping Sally off her feet and into his bed, and talking marriage once they'd assuaged their appetites, he'd launched a more conventional courtship.

By now, his patience should be reaping rewards. Yet despite his constant attendance, the woman still refused to respond to his overtures.

It was as if she didn't even realize he *was* courting her. Worse, she treated him like a junior, when at most there must only be three or four years between them.

Sally seemed to suffer from a curious blindness

when she looked at him. Even that revealing discussion, at times veering toward the combative, at the Pascal wedding hadn't alerted her to how much Charles Kinglake wanted her.

When he'd been a whisker from ignoring their audience and snatching her up in his arms and kissing her until she saw only him.

Several times he'd verged on declaring himself, but Sally remained so unaware of him as a man—of herself as his future bride—that he'd held back. A rash declaration was likely to shatter the friendship they'd established. She might even decide to send him away.

Hell, he'd never been afraid of anything, but he was bloody terrified at the thought of not seeing her every day.

Because while she'd blithely disregarded his every effort to deepen the connection, he'd just fallen more in love with her. Now the idea of living without her was beyond bearing.

What an infernal mess.

A burst of applause crashed through his brooding. For the sake of appearances, he clapped, too.

"Thank you so much for inviting us, Sir Charles." Sally turned to him, her eyes alight with pleasure. She looked particularly pretty tonight, in a stylish rose pink silk gown and with her dark blonde hair dressed with pearls. "Isn't Strozzi marvelous?"

"Yes, marvelous," he said, although he hadn't heard a note. He stared deep into Sally's eyes, seeking some sign, even the smallest spark, that mirrored the inferno devouring him.

A futile quest, damn it. It always was.

"I still don't understand why they don't speak English so a body knows what they're caterwauling about," Anthony Townsend, Earl of Kenwick, said in his thick Yorkshire accent from the chair behind Charles.

"You confessed last week you enjoyed the opera." Kenwick's delicate wife, Fenella, cast him a wry glance. "You're laying the yokel act on a little too thick, my love. I can hear the thud of hobnail boots marching down the cobbles toward us."

Kenwick was an imposing cove—Charles worried about the long-term health of the spindly chair he sat in—so his sheepish expression looked incongruous on his large, blunt features. "Well, aye, a bloke has a certain reputation to uphold."

Everyone in London knew that the Kenwicks adored each other. Charles hoped—not with any great optimism, given his current progress—that he and Sally might one day be as happy.

"As a Philistine?" his wife asked sweetly.

"As a man's man, my darling."

Fenella barely contained a snort of disdain, while Charles turned to Meg. If he looked at Sally right now, he didn't trust himself not to grab her. These opera boxes were deuced constricted when a man had to keep his hands to himself. "Are you enjoying the opera, Miss Ridgeway?"

"Yes, thank you, Sir Charles," she said politely.

Despite his turmoil, his lips twitched at her lukewarm enthusiasm. "But you'd rather be driving Brandon Deerham's bays."

"Rather." As always at the mention of horses, Meg brightened. "They're the most dashing high steppers and respond like angels to the reins."

"Meg," Sally said in reproof. "That's hardly well mannered, when Sir Charles has arranged this treat for you."

Meg's glance at her aunt indicated that her idea of a treat was a little off target. Charles thoroughly approved of Meg, who was cheerful and sensible and clearly loved her aunt. Loving Sally was a major point in her favor, in his admittedly biased opinion. She was a very pretty girl, and much more in the conventional style than her aunt. Rich mahogany hair, large blue eyes shining with life.

Meg was awake to his intentions, even if her aunt wasn't. During their outings, she offered unspoken cooperation in stepping back to allow him to talk to Sally. And he appreciated the girl's willingness to attend concerts and art exhibitions that she had no interest in, so that Sally and he had at least a whisper of a chaperone.

Not that he'd managed to lure Sally into anything improper. More was the blasted pity.

"I'm sorry, Sir Charles," Meg said dutifully, then turned to welcome a party of her friends, including Carey Townsend and Sir Brandon Deerham, who entered the box. This lively crowd was much more Meg's style than Mozart. The footman who arrived with a tray of champagne had trouble making his way through the chattering young people.

"Take your frolics outside into the corridor, Brand and Carey," Kenwick told his stepson and nephew, his deep voice effortlessly cutting through the hubbub. "You lot are noisier than that blasted screeching female we've had to endure for the last hour."

After Meg and her friends had retreated behind a closed door, Charles accepted a glass of champagne. He turned back to Sally who had shifted her chair so she could talk to the Kenwicks.

"Are you still engaged for the few days in the country next week?" Devil take it, he hoped so.

"Yes, Meg and I will be there."

Thank God. Charles wasn't the only man in the ton to notice that the widowed Lady Norwood was a gem. So far there was some consolation in knowing that while he'd had no success capturing her interest, neither had any of the rest of her swains.

Charles lived in fear that some other blockhead might reach Sally in a way he'd never managed. He didn't want to be out of Town for a week with Lord and Lady West, while she remained behind at the mercy of London's eligibles.

"Meg is in alt at the prospect of spending a couple of days in the Wests' stables," Lady Kenwick said, sipping her champagne.

Charles noticed Sally shoot her friend a repressive glance, although why she was annoyed, he couldn't imagine. It wasn't as if Meg's penchant for all things equine was any secret.

"She'll have time to play the young lady, too," Sally said. "This craze for horses is something most girls grow out of well before they become wives and mothers."

"I reckon the lass is more stalwart than that, Sally," Kenwick said. "She's not a bairn who wants a pony on a whim. She's the only person I've ever met whose knowledge of bloodlines and track form vies with West's. Is this your first visit to Shelton Abbey, Kinglake?"

"Yes. I'm very much looking forward to seeing Lord West's collection of Italian masters," Charles said.

A previous Baron West had returned from his grand tour with a ship hold packed with Utrillos and Bronzinos and Caravaggios. Perhaps Charles might persuade West to part with one or two. Like Meg, the current Lord West was more interested in saddle horses than Salvatore Rosas.

"Meg has learned a great deal about art since she's been in London, Sir Charles," Sally said, with more of that blasted easy friendliness. "Largely thanks to you."

Lady Kenwick regarded Sally with disbelief. "Not as

far as I can see. She mistook Silas's Botticelli for a Gainsborough yesterday. Oh!"

Lady Kenwick started in her seat and spilled champagne over her pretty blue gown.

Charles regarded her in consternation. "Are you well, Lady Kenwick?"

As she fumbled for her handkerchief and batted off Kenwick's attempts to help, she shot Sally a killing glance. The fierce expression didn't fit her gentle features. "Yes, quite well, thank you."

"Anyone can make a mistake when it comes to paintings," Sally said staunchly, pulling her handkerchief from her reticule and passing it to her friend to soak up the few drops. "Why, just the other day, Meg was begging me to take her back to the Royal Academy."

That surprised Charles. From what he'd seen, the girl found pictures as dull as opera. "Actually if she's developed any fondness for art, it's due to you, Lady Norwood. You have such interesting and perceptive opinions."

"Thank you," she said. "Love of art runs in the family."

"Sally…" Lady Kenwick began, but Sally spoke over her.

"Is that Miss Veivers over there with Lord Parry? I heard rumors of an offer in the wind."

Without much interest, Charles glanced at the box

opposite. "Surely not. He must be forty years older than she is."

Sally shrugged. "It's customary for the groom to be older than his bride."

"Not that much older."

"Her mother has pushed her at him, poor lamb," Lady Kenwick said. "He's a marquess, after all."

"A marquess without two pennies to rub together," Kenwick said flatly.

"She's rich," Lady Kenwick said.

"What an unholy alliance." Charles felt genuinely sorry for the pretty little girl in the over-decorated gown, sitting between a dissipated roué and a woman with a thrusting chin and a bosom like the prow of a ship.

Sally had been married young to a much older man. Had she, too, accompanied an unwelcome suitor, wearing just such a frozen, frightened look on her youthful features? She never said anything about her marriage, but Charles couldn't help thinking that her set against another husband was rooted in her feelings about Lord Norwood.

Meg returned to the box, interrupting his reflections, and immediately began to chatter about a plan to picnic in Richmond tomorrow.

"Why on earth did you kick me like that?" Fenella

whispered, as they made their way through the throng after the opera. Ahead of Sally and Fenella, Anthony and Sir Charles were discussing the performance. Out of earshot, fortunately, especially in this bedlam.

Still, Sally slowed her steps. "You said Meg was interested in horses."

"She is." Fenella's expression indicated she thought Sally had lost her mind. It was unpleasantly reminiscent of Helena's manner at Amy's wedding.

Sally frowned and turned to check where Meg was. The girl lingered behind with Carey and Brand, but caught her aunt's eye and nodded to indicate that she did her best to make headway. "But Sir Charles is interested in art."

"Yes."

Sally made a frustrated sound. "I don't want him thinking she's a countrified hoyden who spends her life in the stables."

"He's a clever man. I suspect he already knows." Fen paused. "Well, not the countrified hoyden part. You've done a marvelous job teaching her how to go about in society. But the stables part is definitely true."

"Fen, use your head. He won't propose if he thinks her idea of bliss is mucking out a filthy stall."

Fen still didn't seem to understand. Which was odd. She was a smart woman. "But that is her idea of bliss."

Sally bit back another growl. When Fenella's daughter grew up and started looking for a husband, she'd understand. "I know that."

"And she only likes art if it's a painting of a horse."

"She can learn."

"I don't think she wants to." Someone pushed past them, and Fen used the moment to pull Sally into a corner. "Has Meg set her cap at Sir Charles?"

"I think it would be a good match—and he likes her."

"Of course he does. She's very likable. But he's too old for her."

"He's less than ten years her senior. I was twenty years younger than Norwood when we married."

Fenella's expression remained unimpressed. "Well, we know how that turned out."

"You've heard gossip?" Sally asked shakily. Feeling faint, she placed one hand on the wall beside her. She never confided in anyone about her unhappy marriage.

Norwood hadn't been violent, but he'd been over-bearing, uncouth, and perpetually unfaithful. Even as a girl, she couldn't bear the idea of anyone feeling sorry for her. So through the whole humiliating experience, she'd done her best to pretend everything was fine.

"You've gone as white as a sheet." Fenella, always sensitive to others' feelings, reached out to take her gloved hand and squeeze it. "No, I haven't heard anything."

"Then why did you say that?" Sally tugged free.

Compassion softened Fen's gaze to misty blue. "Sally, I've watched your face when people mention your husband. It speaks volumes to anyone with the eyes to see."

"Well, you're mistaken," Sally said sharply. As usual when she recalled her ten years of marriage, shame as heavy as lead crashed down on her.

She'd failed to bear Norwood a child. She'd failed to make him happy. She'd failed to keep him away from other women's beds.

She'd just…failed.

"I'm sure," Fen said, but that damned compassion remained.

Sally swallowed and returned to the principal subject of discussion. "Meg and Sir Charles will be wonderful together."

"In worldly terms, perhaps. But they have nothing in common."

Sally bristled and wished she could kick Fenella again. "He clearly doesn't agree. Or else he wouldn't have dangled after her these last weeks."

"Sally…" Then surprisingly Fenella fell silent.

Sally went on before Fenella could raise any more fiddling objections. "He's kind and steady, and his manners are lovely. And he's handsome enough to set any girl's heart fluttering. He turns heads wherever he goes."

"Yes, he does."

"So Meg would be lucky to catch him."

"Do you think she's in love with him?"

Sally frowned. "She should be."

Fen sighed. "Life doesn't work that way, Sally. Affection falls where it will. 'Should' is a word the heart doesn't understand."

"Well, it should," Sally said crossly.

To her surprise, Fenella laughed. The silvery sound floated above the chatter and attracted Anthony's attention.

He turned back to see what was delaying his wife and her friend. He was so massively tall that he towered over the surging crowd and found them without difficulty. When he sent his wife a rueful smile brimming with unspoken love, Sally's heart twisted with envy. It was painful to witness the Kenwicks' happiness so soon after the reminder of her wretched marriage.

"Sally, you're hopeless," Fenella said with such fondness in her voice, it was difficult for Sally to cling to her annoyance.

Still, her tone was cool as she replied. "Pardon me for trying to set my niece up with a good man."

"You mean well, I know."

"How much more patronizing can you be, Fen? Don't you like Sir Charles?"

"Of course I do." Fenella didn't take offense at Sally's quarrelsome response. "He's charming."

"So?"

"So nothing at all. Meg and he would be a complete disaster together."

"I don't agree," Sally said, stiff-lipped with anger. And a niggling worry she didn't want to acknowledge.

Dear heaven, what if Fen was right? She hadn't taken the trouble to ask her niece how she felt about Sir Charles—she didn't want to arouse expectations when he still might fall from the saddle before the last fence.

Oh, no, now she started to sound like horse-mad Meg.

Fenella, always more inclined toward peacemaking than conflict, said calmly, "You know your niece better than I do, of course."

"Yes, I do."

But she wasn't totally convinced. She and Meg got along, and she loved the girl. But Meg was unusually independent and even at this age, tended to play her own game. She and her aunt didn't indulge in intimate cozes, where Meg poured out her heart and sought her elder's advice.

In fact, although Sally would never admit it aloud, she sometimes wondered if her niece was more worldly wise than she was.

Ridiculous.

But as she moved back into the bustling crowd and checked behind her to make sure Meg was following, she pondered. Did Meg love Sir Charles? He was all that the world admired in a gentleman. And the girl had never expressed any dislike for him.

But did she love him?

Surely she did. If Sally had been an eighteen-year-old girl, and such a wonderful man showed an interest in her, she'd have been in alt.

But Fenella understood people. And Fenella had sounded so certain when she dismissed the idea of Sir Charles and Meg making a happy match. Sally's responsibilities as an aunt had never weighed so heavy.

From the first, she'd done her best to promote Sir Charles's suit. But if there was no hope of it reaching its proper end, had she neglected the girl's other matrimonial chances?

Meg was only eighteen, and her parents weren't desperate for her to wed yet, especially when Sally bore the season's expenses. But still…

If Sir Charles wasn't Meg's choice, did she prefer another suitor? She liked Brand and Carcy, but Sir Charles was right when he'd said the boys were too young to marry. Sally's instincts were that the trio were friends, rather than anything more romantic.

But now it seemed her instincts about her niece were radically opposed to Fenella's.

She looked ahead to where Sir Charles and Anthony waited near the entrance. The light shone down on Sir Charles's rich brown hair and illuminated his classic profile. With a strange little shiver, Sally thought again how attractive he was. Dressed formally for the opera, he was a man to take a girl's breath away.

Meg *must* want to marry him.

As if he sensed her attention, he glanced up and

smiled. She loved watching the way his features softened and those dimples appeared in his cheeks. How
could Meg resist him?

Despite her disquiet, she returned his smile and felt
her certainty flow back. Good heavens, she was
worrying about nothing. There was no reason to doubt
herself.

Fenella was wrong. Meg liked Sir Charles. Sir
Charles liked her. Sally knew that, if for no other
reason than that he took the trouble to be nice to her
aunt. Within the next few weeks, he would propose,
and Meg would end her season in triumph.

Which meant Sally, free of her responsibilities to
her niece, could go on to fulfilling a few plans of her
own. Perhaps buying a permanent home in London.
Taking a lover. Returning to her charity work.

The fact that, right now, all of those things seemed
vilely empty was neither here nor there.

CHAPTER FOUR

*S*ince meeting Morwenna on the committee of a naval charity in Portsmouth, Sally had stayed several times at Shelton Abbey, Lord West's beautiful estate in the Leicestershire countryside. In recent years, her friendship with Morwenna had expanded to encompass all the Nashes and their circle. She loved each of them, especially the original Dashing Widows, Silas's wife Caroline, gentle Fenella, and sardonic, brilliant Helena, her hostess this week.

When Helena invited Sally and Meg to stay as a brief respite from the whirl of the season, she'd been quick to accept. Even more delightful, Helena included Meg's suitor, Sir Charles Kinglake in the party.

Perhaps in a smaller, intimate gathering away from London's distractions, he'd finally offer for her niece. He must have courtship in mind, or else why accept the invitation? While he got along well with Helena and

West—she'd observed he got along well with most people—they weren't particularly close.

Sally had approached the house party, anticipating both her own enjoyment and a happy outcome for Meg and her beau.

But so far, four days into the visit, Shelton Abbey's charms had failed to work their usual magic on her spirits. Sally felt discontented and unsettled. And the worst of it was that she wasn't sure why.

Oh, the causes behind some of her grumbles were obvious. Sir Charles hadn't yet proposed. Even if he did, he'd need to seek Meg in the stables, because the girl had devoted much more attention to Lord West's thoroughbreds than to her future husband.

Sally hadn't been sleeping well, and when she did sleep, odd dreams tormented her. Shaking and breathless, she'd open her eyes to darkness, with vague memories of running down endless corridors in search of something she never found. Last night, Caro had commented on her uncharacteristic distraction.

Now she sat on a red lacquer bench in the charming Chinese pavilion, trying to puzzle out the source of her fretfulness, a fretfulness that had started with Amy's wedding nearly a fortnight ago.

Mercifully she was alone. The rest of the party, including eight energetic children, had taken an excursion to a local beauty spot. But she'd cried off, saying she had letters to write. This urge for her own company wasn't her usual style either.

Generally she was an even-tempered creature, willing to make the best of circumstances. Through charity work, she'd even managed to find some purpose through the endless years of her marriage. She was someone who held her head high through any storm.

Except now there was no storm, and she had no real troubles. Yet yesterday, when she'd broken a vase in her room, she'd burst into tears like a hysterical girl.

"So you dodged the trip to the castle ruins with the children, too?"

The deep voice startled her, made every nerve tighten. Sally straightened and surreptitiously wiped away the few tears she'd shed, watching the late afternoon light over the lovely rose garden before her.

For a sensible, equable lady past first youth, she was acting more like a dizzy adolescent than Meg ever did. Even as a girl, she couldn't remember crying over a sunset like a sappy heroine in a Minerva Press novel.

"Sir Charles, you caught me unawares." As she cursed the husky edge to her voice, she tried to read his expression. But even in the wilds of Leicestershire, Sir Charles Kinglake's perfect urbanity remained impenetrable.

She felt the familiar surge of admiration at the sight of him. He was casually dressed in a bottle green coat and buff breeches. The faint breeze ruffled his thick brown hair where the long rays of light discovered rich russet highlights.

He didn't look like the elegant London gentleman who had escorted Meg and her chaperone to balls and the theatre. He looked in his element, as if the country suited him.

She must still be suffering the aftereffects of his unexpected appearance. Her heart was racing so fast that her breath caught.

"I'm sorry." That very nice smile appeared, as did the charming dimples. "I've been here a few minutes, but you were so lost to your thoughts, you didn't notice."

Damn and blast. Had he seen her crying?

She plastered a bright expression on her face. "I was thinking how lovely it is here."

"It is indeed." Those attractive laughter lines deepened around his eyes. "Although anything that doesn't involve four legs, a tail and a whinny looks good to me at the moment."

She mustered a laugh at his disgusted tone, but her inexplicable edginess lingered.

Not that she could blame him for tiring of the company. So far, the talk had been very…equine.

Meg and Brand and Carey directed discussion toward horsey matters at any opportunity—and given Helena and West bred the best horses in England, opportunities had been numerous. Silas and Caro made some attempt to shift the focus, but with little success.

If Fenella were here, Sally would owe her an apology. It had been a complete waste of time, trying to hide Meg's monomania from Sir Charles.

"Don't you like horses?" she asked curiously.

Norwood had considered himself a great expert on horses. Actually Norwood had considered himself a great expert on everything under God's heaven. The thought of her late, unlamented husband reminded her how much she liked Sir Charles, who spoke to her as if she had a brain between her ears.

Sir Charles ambled across to sit beside her and stretch his long, booted legs out across the tiles with their red and white chinoiserie design. That inexplicable catch in her breath was back. If the evening had been cold, she might understand it. But it was perfect weather for late spring.

He sighed. "Not for breakfast, lunch and dinner."

"Has it been very dull for you?" Without thinking, she placed her hand on his. At the contact, a strange frisson tingled along her arm.

All her earlier awkwardness rushed back, and she snatched her hand away to set it trembling in her lap. She really was acting like an idiot. Perhaps when she returned to London, she should consult her doctor.

Sir Charles surveyed her thoughtfully. "There have been some compensations."

Ridiculously Sally found herself blushing. She couldn't remember the last time she'd blushed. Before her marriage surely.

She hurried into speech. "I promise you that Meg

does talk about other things. I think she's just so excited to see all these champions in one place."

To her relief, Sir Charles shifted that enigmatic brown gaze from her to the gardens. Sally immediately sucked in a deep breath to feed her starved lungs. For some reason, she'd felt quite lightheaded when he stared into her eyes.

"There's no doubt she's happy."

"Ecstatic," Sally said drily. No point pretending anything different, she admitted. At least Sir Charles didn't sound particularly put out to run a distant second to West's most recent Derby winner in the girl's estimation. "Have you managed to ferret out West's art collection? You said you were looking forward to seeing it."

"I visited the pictures in the long gallery the day after I arrived, although they deserve a second look. Have you seen them?"

His good-humored interest should put her at ease. But her heart still skipped around like a grasshopper, and she felt unaccountably nervy in his presence.

"Not recently. I must admit when I come to Shelton Abbey, I spend most of my time gossiping with Helena and her friends. We all live so far apart. It's nice to have a chance to talk fashion and scandal and family news." She made an apologetic gesture. "You'll think I'm hopelessly frivolous."

This visit, she'd avoided those cozy chats. She didn't want to face questions about this restless mood she was in—and she knew both Helena and Caro had noticed that she wasn't her cheerful, chatty self.

When he smiled, the kindness in his eyes made her think yet again what a nice man he was. "As long as you aren't gossiping about horses, I have no criticism."

It was her turn to laugh, surprised that it came out quite easily. "Meg and the boys have added a different flavor to the visit."

"A whiff of hay and harnesses?"

"Exactly."

He stood and presented his arm. "Would you like to go inside and wander through the West collection with me? We have the manor to ourselves—no children playing blind man's buff in the gallery, no horse-mad youth, desperate to discuss fetlocks and snaffle bits."

Over the weeks she'd known Sir Charles, they'd spent many enjoyable hours touring London's galleries, public and private. Meg had accompanied them good naturedly, but without showing much interest in the art.

Lord Norwood had been a sporting gentleman who scorned his wife's cultivated tastes. Sally had loved talking to someone intelligent and well informed, who shared her love of beautiful things. In truth, Sir Charles was much more well informed than she was. And unlike many of the ton's connoisseurs, he didn't speak down to her as a mere woman. His genuine interest in her opinions had helped her confidence to blossom.

"I rather think I would." She smiled up at him and

rose to accept his arm. That odd little shiver rippled through her again, but this time she ignored it. The reaction must just be one more symptom of her recent distraction.

The next day, the weather changed for the worse, and everyone was confined inside, much to the chagrin of the horsier members of the party. In the afternoon, most of the guests played cards, or wrote letters, or joined in a riotous game of skittles with the children in the long gallery.

Charles had sought refuge in West's library—as he'd predicted, well-stocked with books about horses. Now he stood at the window, watching the pouring rain and wondering where Sally was. Since their tour of the long gallery, she'd proven elusive. She wasn't with the others. He'd hoped he might find her in here, but the room was empty.

These last days, she wasn't acting like herself, and he was worried that it boded ill for his courtship. When he'd discovered her in the rose garden, she'd seemed unusually self-conscious and ill at ease.

For once, they'd been gloriously alone. Ah, if only she'd accept his advances, the setting had been perfect for romance. But some instinct had stopped him from kissing her. With every day, it became more difficult to hide his hunger, but he'd managed to resist temptation. Barely.

Sally moved through the world sheltered behind an oddly unbreakable shell of isolation. One might almost imagine she was a beautiful painting herself, and not warm, human flesh, ripe for a man's touch.

If she hadn't been married nearly ten years, Charles would almost call her lack of awareness innocence.

"Is this where you're hiding, old man?" Silas Nash, Lord Stone, strode through the door with his usual energy, leaving it ajar behind him. Beneath the thatch of light brown hair, his features were alight with humor and intelligence.

Charles turned, grateful that someone interrupted his brooding. He liked Stone. He liked all the Nashes and their connections. And he positively envied Stone's marriage to vivid, lovely Caroline. Eight years and four children had done nothing to cool the heat between them.

The nurseries upstairs were packed with the next generation of Nashes and Granges. Stone and Caro had brought their children, as well as Morwenna's four-year-old daughter Kerenza, to Shelton Abbey to play with their three cousins.

"I came for a book." And to track down one lovely Dashing Widow.

Stone joined him at the window and stared out at the gray landscape. "And to escape the horsey set, I'll wager."

Charles's smile was wry. "That, too."

"Nash offspring are flung onto their first pony before they can walk. But I must say even I have reached the limit of my interest in thoroughbred antecedents. Meg and West and the boys had gone back as far as the Byerley Turk, when I left the morning room in search of more sensible conversation."

"I hope you've found it," Charles said with a smile. "What are you working on at the moment?"

"A dwarf version of Caro's tree for people who don't have room for a bloody great orchard." The "Caroline Nash" cherry tree he released a few years after his marriage had caused a sensation in horticultural circles.

"How is it going?"

Stone's lips twitched. "Will it sound like a bad joke if I say I'm making *small* progress?"

"Yes."

"Excellent." His tone turned serious. "We're actually at a critical point in the grafting. I hope in the master's absence, my army of assistants back at Woodley Park are watching the shoots and not breaking into the wine cellars."

"So why did you come to Shelton Abbey?"

Stone shrugged without resentment. "Caro and Helena haven't had much time together over the last months, at least time away from the social world. And the children were clamoring to see their cousins.

Family is more important than a cherry tree, however fine, even if I do say so myself."

Charles's envy of this man's domestic contentment sharpened until it tasted like rust on his tongue. This, this was what Charles wanted. With Sally Cowan. Love. A passionate connection with a lovely woman. Children. A home where he found purpose and joy.

Yet Sally persisted in treating him like an acquaintance. It was enough to make a man want to join Stone's unsupervised assistants and raid the claret cellar.

"I'm sure. Even horse-mad sisters."

Stone nodded. "Even horse-mad sisters. Hel's always been avid for the nags. It was something she and West had in common when they were young. I'm devilish glad they found their way back to each other."

Charles eyed Stone in the flat gray light. "By God, you're a romantic."

Stone gave another shrug. "Life's made me one."

"You're lucky."

"I am indeed." Stone's smile expressed what he didn't say. But Charles had witnessed the soul-deep happiness in his family and didn't need any explanation.

Stone surveyed Charles from under his brows, as if unsure whether he should continue. "You know, you could be lucky, too."

Charles frowned, although he wasn't surprised Stone had noticed his interest in Sally. The Nashes were a notoriously clever family, and not just with horses and horticulture. "You've guessed that I'm contemplating matrimony?"

"It's reasonably obvious, at least to a fellow who's languished in just your situation."

"I'm not sure the lady returns my interest."

"Poor devil, I remember that feeling. It was damned wretched." Stone sent him a straight look. "Of course, there's only one way to find out whether you're wasting your time. You need to declare yourself. Unless you mean to yearn after her until you're both old and gray."

Charles gave a twisted smile. "I never knew the meaning of terror until I set out to win a bride."

Stone clapped him on the back. "Worse than facing a loaded pistol at twenty paces. But worth it in the long run."

"Only if she says yes."

"You're a persuasive fellow. You'll get your way in the end—and my advice is make your move while you're down here. Fewer distractions."

Charles had to laugh. "Are you saying my proposal isn't interesting enough to capture the lady's attention?"

"Heaven forbid, old chum. No, I'm saying that Shelton Abbey is full of isolated corners inside and out that a man can use to…make his point with a lady he fancies. And if you haven't worked that out already, I'm a Dutchman."

Charles had worked it out. Yesterday alone in the rose garden with Sally—and again in the deserted long gallery—she'd only just escaped a thorough kissing. But that damned air of fragility had stopped him.

"You know," he said slowly, "I'm going about this all wrong. The subtle approach isn't getting me anywhere. A siege might be called for, after all."

Stone's smile reeked delight. "That's the spirit. I tried something similar to your slow burn pursuit with Caro, and nearly lost her to bloody West as a result. I remember how putting myself on the line scared me silly—but it won me my bride, so it was worth every collywobble."

Charles frowned thoughtfully out into the rain. Was Stone right? Excitement bubbled in his veins as he imagined finally having Sally in his arms.

Perhaps it was time to shock her into seeing him as a husband.

He turned back to Stone who watched him with an unwavering gaze. "So Caro said yes when you declared yourself, and you lived happily ever after?"

Stone snorted with derision. "Not a bit of it, old man. She sent me away with a flea in my ear and told me she never wanted to see me again. I was convinced all was lost."

"Hell's bells," Charles muttered.

"Worst day of my life. But I persevered, and eventually she relented. Even then, it took months to persuade her to marry me. With a widow, there's sometimes the problem of once bitten, twice shy."

Charles had long ago guessed that Sally's silence about her marriage hinted at unhealed wounds. But Norwood had died four years ago. It was time for her to find new happiness.

With a surge of determination, he straightened and met Stone's bright hazel eyes. "I'm going to propose to the girl and shame the devil. Then let the dice fall where they may."

"Good show." Stone's smile radiated approval. "And I wish you the devil's own luck, my friend."

CHAPTER FIVE

*S*ally reeled back from the library door, open a crack so she'd clearly heard the conversation inside. Her heart was racing, and a jagged boulder blocked her throat. Hot tears stung her eyes, so she saw the elegant corridor with its graceful side tables and Chinese pottery through a misty haze.

She'd wanted a book, but paused before entering the library when she realized Silas and Sir Charles were in the midst of a discussion. Before she'd decided whether to interrupt or not, what she heard made her curious.

Eavesdropping was beyond the pale. And she suffered the fabled fate of eavesdroppers—she didn't like what she heard.

She stumbled toward the drawing room. With shaking hands, she pushed open the door and said a fervent prayer of thanks to find it unoccupied. Biting her lip to stifle a sob, she shut the door behind her and rested back on it, trembling.

At last, Sir Charles had stated his intention to propose to Meg. It shouldn't come as a surprise—it didn't. Although his diffidence about his reception was unexpected. Sally had feared she'd been too obvious in her matchmaking, and if perhaps that had contributed to his tardiness in coming up to scratch.

Yet today, when she heard him say he'd set his sights on Meg, she wanted to die.

Because now when there was no longer any doubt that he hoped to marry her niece, Sally discovered that she wanted Sir Charles Kinglake for herself.

What a mess.

What a disaster.

And what a blind fool she'd been.

She'd survived her cold marriage by locking away her longing heart. She'd done this so successfully that she'd assumed all deeper emotion was forever banished from her life.

Whereas it turned out she was wrong, and her heart had only been sleeping. Now that understanding descended like a thunderclap, she realized her heart had clamored for her attention for weeks. But she'd been deaf to its frantic messages.

Obstinately deaf.

Any woman of sense would know that female interest sparked her pleasure in Sir Charles's company. And see the stirrings of attraction in her erratic pulse in his presence. And know that she was constantly unhappy and restless because she wanted him.

Anyone but silly Sally Cowan, that is.

Anyone but a woman who had never known desire.

No wonder she didn't recognize desire when it came to life.

Desire. And...love.

Because the devastating truth was that she wasn't too old to fall in love. She loved Sir Charles more with every breath she took. He was everything she'd ever wanted in a man.

And he was completely out of reach.

She gulped in a huge breath of air and placed a shaking hand over her heaving stomach. She could cry now in private. But she must put on a brave face when the engagement was announced.

She should be used to maintaining a show, after her years with Norwood, acting as if everything was fine.

But somehow this was different. Worse. Far more painful, however miserable her marriage had been. This unwelcome, overwhelming love for a man she could never have must remain her secret.

She'd always valued the easy honesty of her dealings with Sir Charles. In the eight weeks since he'd been in London, they'd become friends. Now as a mere friend, she'd assume a cheerful air when he wed Meg. Who was a lovely girl and who deserved this paragon of a man.

No doubt they'd be terrifically happy.

The idea of that terrific happiness made her want to scream.

With a choked sob, she fumbled to lock the door. Her hands were all thumbs, but she managed it at last, thank heaven. Then she staggered across the carpet and collapsed into an armchair. Useless tears burned her eyes like acid, but right now, when she needn't pretend to be anything but bitterly unhappy, she gave way to the luxury of a good cry.

Because she was doubly shut out of paradise. Even if Sir Charles didn't want to marry Meg, he'd never court a barren widow several years his senior. He'd want someone young and sweet—and damn it, fertile. Any man would.

She could cry now, but once she left this room, she must gather herself up. She must act as if nothing was the matter, and she was delighted the man she loved was marrying her niece. After all, she'd promoted the match from the start. Pride, duty, and affection for Meg all mandated that she held her head high and smiled and smiled and smiled.

She clenched her fists against the chair's arms. How in the name of all that was holy could she endure it?

Charles approached dinner, determined to stake his claim with Sally. Once formalities were done, he intended to take his beloved on a candlelit tour of the long gallery. A tour that he planned to end with kisses and joy and her promise to become his wife.

But from the moment everyone gathered in the drawing room, he noticed that Sally was different. Hard and glittering—and arch in a way he'd never seen her before.

He usually despised archness, but in Sally, the flirtatious gaiety just made him want her more than ever. He itched to give her a good shake and kiss her, until that coquettish expression melted into surrender. And rip that spectacular silvery dress from her long slender body and plunge deep inside her until at last she saw him and nobody else.

Because however her behavior vexed him, he couldn't deny she looked magnificent, with a hard sparkle that made him think of diamonds. While the silvery dress inevitably reminded him of armor.

Just what did she need armor against? An unwelcome suitor called Charles Kinglake?

He couldn't help thinking that was the answer. And that made him itch to smash something. Never once did she look in his direction. Even when he wished her good evening, she responded to a spot over his right shoulder.

He wasn't alone in noticing something amiss.

"Sally, that's a gorgeous dress, but it's making the rest of us feel distinctly underdone," Helena said from near the unlit fire, where she stood with her brother Stone. It was warm for May, and the French doors stood open to the fragrant evening. "Are we expecting a royal visit I don't know about?"

Sally laughed. Was Charles the only one to hear the edge of hysteria in the sound? "My *modiste* finished it last week, and I decided I couldn't wait to wear it."

Helena's lips adopted a wry twist. "If I'd known we were going formal, I'd have worn my diamonds."

"You don't need diamonds to shine, my love," West said. He and Caroline were chatting on a chaise longue against the wall.

"Oh, you should never say that to a lady," Sally said with a flirtatious glance at her host. Meg, who as usual was talking about horses with Brandon and Carey, cast her aunt a glance weighted with concern.

Charles frowned. Something was horribly wrong, but he had no idea what the devil it could be. Sally was trying too hard to shine. Her natural vivacity turned to brittleness. She was noticeably a different creature from the woman he knew.

He wished everyone else in the room to Hades. Damn manners and propriety. He wanted to confront her and find out what had changed. But social rules made that impossible.

Yet again, his lack of status in Sally's life stung. The unwelcome truth was that she could walk away from him tomorrow, and he'd have no right to call her back.

In the world's eyes, they were mere acquaintances. Whereas in his eyes, she was the center of his world.

"None of you gorgeous creatures needs diamonds

to shine." West, who had had a career in diplomatic circles before he married his childhood sweetheart, sent his wife a fond smile. "You all sparkle like the stars anyway."

Helena's expression turned sardonic. "Nicely saved, my dear. But don't imagine that means you're getting back the necklace you gave me for Christmas."

Caroline smiled. "And while we mightn't need diamonds, never imagine we don't want them."

Stone groaned theatrically. "See what you've done, Sally? Now I'm stuck with another trip to Rundell and Bridge. After the last one, I had to mortgage the estate."

The lovely brunette in spring green fluttered her eyelashes at her husband. "I'm sure it was worth every penny, my love."

Stone placed a tragic hand to his brow. "What does it matter if I feed our children on stale bread and water, as long as their mother's taste for baubles is satisfied?"

"See?" Helena turned to West. "That's the right attitude. You could learn a lot from my brother."

Stone, rich enough to bedeck a hundred wives in diamonds, directed a woebegone look at his best friend. "You never think before you speak, do you, old man?"

West's expression held a hint of smugness. "No need to thank me, chum."

"Then I won't."

"Sir Charles, see what you've got to look forward to when you take a wife?" Helena said.

Sally was still avoiding looking at him. He struggled to hide his disquiet and raised his glass to his lovely hostess who, while not as elaborately dressed as Sally, was stylish in teal silk. "Apparently a lifetime of buying diamonds."

"Oh, you're going to make some lucky woman a wonderful husband," Caro said, sending Stone a sly look.

"I do hope so," Charles said, but his hard-won smile faded when out of the corner of his eye, he caught Sally's unguarded expression. The glitter had disappeared as if it had never been. Instead she looked stricken and pale, and her eyes were dark with misery.

Hell, what did all this mean? Had she somehow guessed he meant to propose tonight and the idea filled her with horror? Dear God, surely that couldn't be the problem.

Sally looked like her best friend had just died. What in creation was the matter? He racked his brains, but he still for the life of him couldn't work out any reason for her behavior.

She caught him looking at her, and she plastered on a smile. But the bitter unhappiness lingered in her eyes.

He loathed seeing her like this. He wanted to battle all her dragons, keep her safe, make her happy. But right now, he fought an invisible enemy.

"Shall we go through to dinner?" Helena gestured to Charles to take her into the dining room.

As the others made up couples, with the exception

of Brandon who sauntered in last, they went through and found their places.

Charles had hoped to sit beside Sally, where he had a chance at a private word, but Helena had placed him on her right. A position of honor certainly—he wished to God he appreciated it.

"Don't give up hope," Helena murmured as he helped her to her seat.

Charles's faint laugh was tinged with displeasure. "What in Hades? Are you all aware of my plans?"

Helena's glance fell on Sally who sat further down the table. She was glittering at Carey who looked appropriately dazzled. "No, I don't think we all are. But you'll get there in the end."

Charles studied his beloved, and couldn't help feeling Helena was overly optimistic. Tonight Sally seemed set on captivating every male here, with the exception of the one who wanted to marry her.

He supposed he should be grateful that the party included two happily married men and a pair of striplings not yet twenty-one. But watching the woman he loved preen and flirt with those two handsome young pups set his teeth on edge.

Charles was grateful that discussion centered on politics when the gentlemen lingered behind for their port. He avoided Stone's meaningful looks and took an extra glass, but the premonition of disaster looming ahead only tangled his gut into tighter knots.

Over dinner, Sally had been witty and incandescent —and she still hadn't looked at him. He'd combed his memory for some way that he'd offended her. But he couldn't think of a thing. When they'd parted after seeing West's art collection, she'd seemed as friendly as ever.

To think, he'd found that cause for complaint.

When the gentlemen joined the ladies in the drawing room, Sally looked up at his entrance, then her gaze slid off him and landed on West and Silas. Charles braced for more blasted glittering, but she remained quiet. And strangely sad, despite the smile fixed to her face. The smile wasn't terribly convincing.

"What do you think this weather is going to do?" Caro asked from the sofa, where she sat beside Helena.

"Spring rain here can settle in and last for days, I'm afraid." West moved forward to rest his hand on his wife's shoulder. Helena glanced up with a soft smile.

Charles ground his teeth. It wasn't the night for him to appreciate other people's marital bliss.

Meg, for once, wasn't talking about horses. Instead she was flicking through a fashion magazine at a table in the corner. Brandon and Carey were absent. Charles guessed they were playing billiards. With great glee, they'd discovered the table this morning. Perhaps that was why Sally was sad—she'd lost her audience for her flirting.

Charles no longer held out any hope of proposing tonight. But he badly wanted to know what had upset Sally, and if he could do anything to help. He hated knowing that despite her show of effervescence, she was wretched.

He smiled at her. "Lady Norwood, I'm keen to see West's Caravaggios by candlelight. Would you like to accompany me?"

"Perhaps not this evening, Sir Charles," Sally said in a dull tone. And while every eye in the room focused on her with varying degrees of curiosity, Sally still talked to someone invisible standing just behind him.

She straightened, and he saw that she was still unusually pale. When she reached out to grip the mantelpiece, her long, slender fingers were rigid with tension.

What the devil? Even more concerned, Charles stepped forward. "Lady Norwood, aren't you well?"

He saw her begin to shake her head, then she gave a jerky nod. "I have a slight headache."

Helena's expression held more speculation than sympathy, Charles noted. "Perhaps it's being cooped up inside all day."

Sally sent her a shaky smile. Hard to believe this was the creature who had scintillated with coruscating brilliance only half an hour ago. Perhaps she was genuinely ill, but the more Charles looked at her, the less he believed it.

No, something had upset her. He just wished to

Hades he knew what it was. The sight of Sally Cowan fighting to contain her distress made him insane. He loathed that she shut him out.

If he'd ever doubted that he loved her, the way he felt now when he saw her unhappy confirmed that he was irrevocably hers.

"I'm sure that's it." Sally went back to addressing Charles's right shoulder. "However I think Meg would love to see the paintings. She has a great enthusiasm for *chiaroscuro.*"

Charles stifled a derisive retort. Not unless Chiaroscuro was the name of a racehorse, she didn't. He waited for Meg to make some excuse.

To his surprise, the girl closed the magazine. "I'd love to."

Good God, the world turned upside down. Charles remembered his manners in time to bow to Meg. "Capital. Shall we?"

He lifted a lit candelabra and offered his arm. Meg stood and curled her hand around his elbow. "We shall."

"Have fun," Sally said after them, and he could swear he heard a crack in her voice.

Puzzled, he glanced back as he and Meg reached the door. For the first time all evening, Sally was staring directly at him.

She was no longer pale. Instead she looked like she suffered a fever. She bit her lip, and her chin trembled.

Growing up with four sisters told him she tried with all her might to hold back tears.

What the hell?

Then she realized he was looking at her, and she dredged up that careless smile, no more convincing than it had been earlier.

The memory of the strain in her piquant face haunted him as he left the drawing room with Meg at his side.

CHAPTER SIX

*M*eg was uncharacteristically quiet as Charles escorted her into the shadowy gallery. They progressed past gilded frames and portraits mysterious in the candlelight to the first Caravaggio. Meg dutifully turned to face the huge canvas, although he'd wager a thousand guineas that the girl wasn't remotely interested in the painting.

"Here it is." He raised the candelabra to reveal the Madonna sorrowing at the foot of the Cross. Mary was lit with bright gold light, while the rest of the desolate landscape lay shrouded in darkness.

Meg studied the sublime painting with a disgruntled expression. "There are no horses."

The response, while predictable, made him laugh. He'd felt so low when he'd left the drawing room, he was surprised that he could. He placed the candelabra on a side table. "You, Miss Meg, are a Philistine."

Transferring her gaze to him, she shrugged. "Of course I am."

He leaned one shoulder against the wall and surveyed her, wondering what she was up to. Because she was undoubtedly up to something.

"So why this sudden interest in West's art collection?" It was a deuced pity that Sally hadn't seen fit to come with him. The silence and isolation were just right for passionate declarations.

Charles stiffened in sudden horror. Good God, was this girl having similar thoughts?

"Dash it all, Miss Meg, you're not expecting something to happen, are you?"

It wasn't the most coherent of questions, but there was nothing wrong with Meg's brain. She understood immediately, and gave a reassuringly contemptuous snort. "Like a proposal? Don't be silly."

He laughed again, too relieved to be offended, and folded his arms. "So why are we here?"

"Because I want to talk to you, and it's almost impossible to get any privacy. Propriety is a devil of a pest."

Charles heartily agreed. If only he'd got Sally alone tonight, he'd have winkled out the cause of her troubles. But as a single man unrelated to her, he had to behave circumspectly. Even here, among friends. "So what is it you want to say?"

Meg's stare intensified. "Aunt Sally thinks you want to marry me."

"What on earth?" Shock made him stand up straight and uncross his arms.

The girl studied him curiously. "Do you want to marry me?"

Biting back the urge to curse like a sailor at this unexpected turn, he shook his head. He felt so nonplused, his answer emerged with more frankness than tact.

"Not a bit of it." He frowned. "Do you want to marry me?"

"No. You're too old for me."

Despite everything, a huff of amusement escaped him. "Well, that puts me in my place."

"I beg your pardon." Meg's blush was visible, even in the candlelight. "That was rude."

"But true." Then the full significance of what Meg had told him deflated all humor. "*Sally* thinks I want to marry you?"

Damn, damn, damn.

Hurt, frustration, and confusion crashed into one another and left him reeling. Don't say he and Sally had been at cross purposes from the beginning. Was this why she didn't respond to his overtures, because she'd consigned him to her charming, but completely incompatible niece?

The idea beggared belief. Surely she knew him better than this. But when he looked at Meg's face, he saw no hint of teasing. Furious disappointment rammed his gut and left him winded.

Meg nodded. "She thinks that's why you've been so attentive."

"Dash it, I've been so attentive because—" He stopped, unsure how much he wanted to reveal to this self-assured chit.

"Because you're in love with Aunt Sally."

"Meg…"

She sent him a sharp look. "Are you going to deny it?"

"Not at all." Feeling as if he'd entered a world where nothing made sense, he crossed to slump into one of the gilt armchairs set opposite the Caravaggio.

"Good." Meg followed him and took the chair beside his.

He hardly knew how to respond. As he examined the unpalatable truth, his stomach churned with angry disbelief. "So that's why she's been so nice to me."

"Don't be a blockhead, Sir Charles. She likes you."

"As a husband for her niece." His voice emerged as a growl. He raised his head and studied Meg. "She doesn't see me as her suitor at all, does she?"

Meg's expression made her look much wiser than her eighteen years warranted. "Don't be angry with her."

"I'm not." Which was a blatant lie. At the moment, he burned to corner Sally and insist that she came to her senses.

"Yes, you are, and I don't blame you. But it's not her fault. I want you to see that."

"How the devil can I see that?"

Meg sighed. "Because I'm going to break a few confidences and tell you things you couldn't know."

He frowned, as curiosity set a brake on his rising temper. "Are you sure?"

"Do you really love her?"

"With every beat of my heart."

"And you want to marry her?"

Despite the moment's seriousness, his lips twisted into a wry smile. "Do you have the right to ask me that?"

Meg shrugged. "She has nobody else to look after her."

"What about your father?"

"He has enough on his plate, with six daughters to marry off. The affairs of his youngest sister come well down on his list of things to worry about. So do you mean marriage?"

"Of course." He sighed, and enough resentment lingered to add an edge to his words. "I hoped she'd come around to my way of thinking in her own time, but I hadn't counted on her asinine plans to marry us off."

"I think if you leave it to Aunt Sally, she'll never come around to the idea that you want to marry her."

"I begin to wonder if you're right." He was starting to realize that a man could bash himself to pieces against the barriers Sally raised against the world and still make no crack in her defenses. "What do you suggest? Pouncing?"

Somewhat to his relief, Meg's giggle brought her back to looking like an eighteen-year-old girl. "It might be something to consider. You're always so careful with her. I've noticed, even if Aunt Sally hasn't."

"It's odd—she's so bright and vital, yet at heart, there's something fragile about her."

"You *are* the right man for her." Meg's smile glowed with approval. "I always thought so, and you just proved it."

"While she thinks I'm right for you," Charles snapped, still stung at how badly Sally had misjudged him.

Meg sighed. "Aunt Sally is clever about people— mostly. But she's completely blind when she looks at herself. She believes she's past the age where romance and marriage are possible."

"I know. She told me. It's so deuced frustrating." With an impatient gesture, he ran his hand through his hair. "She's only thirty-one."

"She's convinced she's too old to attract a husband— at least one who doesn't want a sensible woman to run his house and comfort his last years." Meg's eyes sharpened. "Did you know my late uncle, Lord Norwood?"

"No."

"Lucky you." Her mouth turned down in contempt. "He was an awful man. Dull, stolid, sure he knew best on every matter under the sun. A bore and a bully. I don't know how my aunt lived with him for nearly ten years without coshing him with a fire iron. And he never did much to hide his disappointment about not siring an heir."

"I suppose he blamed Sally." Meg painted a vivid picture of Sally's first husband.

Charles shouldn't be surprised at what he heard. He'd picked up immediately that Sally bore scars from the past. His anger gradually dissipated.

"He never said so in my hearing, although we all knew he did. It speaks volumes for her strength of character that she managed to keep as much spirit as she has."

Poor Sally. Charles had no difficulty understanding how marriage to such a man had damaged her generous soul. Lord Norwood's conceit and crassness would eat away at her sense of herself as worthy of affection. Domestic tyranny was a cruel punishment for such a lively creature.

And there was no escape if a woman believed the marriage vow sacrosanct, as he suspected Sally did. She'd never seek reassurance in another man's arms. Instead she'd endure with as much grace and courage as she could, while loneliness grew and grew, until it threatened to devour her.

Compassion so strong it was like a physical pain gripped him as he imagined her ten years with

Norwood. She couldn't even find consolation in the love of her children. After observing Sally's dealings with Meg and Amy and Morwenna, he knew that the woman he wanted to marry had a huge capacity for love.

It was one of the things he found most powerfully attractive about her.

His anger returned, this time directed at Lord Norwood. "He didn't mistreat her, did he?"

The idea of anyone hurting Sally made his stomach heave. He clenched his hands against the arms of the chair. He wanted to fight dragons for her, but it turned out the dragon blighting her life was dead and eternally out of his reach. Bugger it.

Meg shook her head. "There was no talk in the family that he did. But violence isn't the only cruelty. He used to leave her alone in the country month after month and come up to Town to chase Cyprians. The fatter the better. And if I know that, I'm sure Aunt Sally does."

He frowned at Meg. "You shouldn't understand such things."

She shrugged. "Society acts like young girls have neither ears nor the brains to work out what those ears are hearing. Of course I know about the ladies of Covent Garden and their sisters."

What was the point of disapproval? He shook his head in disbelief at this coil he found himself in. No wonder his courtship hadn't prospered. "If Sally's so willfully blind to her attractions, how the devil is a man to break through to her?"

Meg studied him thoughtfully. "Perhaps pouncing is the way forward."

"I doubt it. Tonight she wouldn't even look at me—and she flirted with every dam…dashed fellow in that room. Every fellow but me."

"Actually that might be a good sign."

He regarded Meg in disbelief. "How the deuce could that be a good sign?"

To his surprise, she reached over and clasped his hand in brief encouragement. "Something has frightened her—I can see that. Can't you?"

He straightened and pulled away. "You're not saying she's scared of me?"

"If she's attracted to you, she would be terrified, I suspect."

He sent her a narrow-eyed look. "You're trying to bolster my confidence."

"I'm trying to tell you not to give up on her—but perhaps change your tactics."

"Pounce?"

Meg nodded firmly. "Pounce."

Charles's response was lost as Helena approached, carrying a candle. "You two have been away a long time."

"We started talking, Lady West." Still struggling to come to terms with what he'd learned tonight, Charles stood at his hostess's arrival. "It's my fault. I should have returned Miss Meg to the drawing room half an hour ago."

"No matter. We're not looking to make a scandal."

He struggled to pin a smile to his face, but it was difficult when his mind was in complete tumult. Marry Meg? What an utterly ludicrous idea. Sally had bats in her belfry. "We'll go and make our peace with her chaperone."

Helena shook her head. "Sally went to bed just after you left. That's why I'm tonight's guardian of propriety."

Meg stood and smoothed the skirts of her yellow silk gown. "I'm sorry we made you come and fetch us, Lady West."

Helena shrugged. "I don't mind. But it's getting late."

"Has everyone retired?" Charles asked.

"Silas and my husband are in the library emptying the brandy decanter and reliving boyhood exploits. Caro has gone upstairs to check on the children. I think Brand and Carey are still playing billiards."

"With your permission, I may linger with the Caravaggio."

"Certainly. Meg?"

"I might go and see how the billiards are progressing," she said and curtsied to Charles. "Good night, Sir Charles."

"Good night, Miss Meg," he said, and hoped she heard his fervent gratitude. By God, he'd been fighting his battle for Sally blindfolded. Now at least he knew what he was up against.

Charles watched the girl leave with Helena, then raised his eyes to the painting before him. But for once, art, however magnificent, couldn't compel his attention. Instead his mind turned over every aspect of that infuriating, astonishing, enlightening discussion with Meg.

He understood so much that had confused him. Sally's curious mixture of confidence and insecurity. The air of innocence, incongruous in a widow in her thirties. Her unwillingness to speak about her marriage.

Poor, poor Sally, trapped in such an uncongenial union. If heaven granted him the privilege, Charles would do all he could to ensure that her second marriage was more to her taste.

If there was a second marriage.

Meg seemed to think he could persuade Sally to marry him. So did Stone. And tonight at dinner, Helena had offered encouragement.

He hoped to hell all of them were right. Hungering after Sally in London had been bad enough. Living with her under one roof, however vast, threatened to drive him out of his head with frustration.

Perhaps he should take Meg's advice. It might be time to... *pounce.*

CHAPTER SEVEN

*S*ally woke late the next morning to the horrid feeling that an unidentified doom was about to crash down over her.

Then she remembered.

Last night, Sir Charles and Meg had gone alone into the long gallery. It was the perfect opportunity to propose.

Her stomach lurched with misery, and she groaned and turned over to bury her head in the pillows. She didn't want to face the world. She didn't want to act pleased for the bride, when instead she wanted to *be* the bride.

No matter how impossible that was, even had Meg not been his choice.

Bitter tears stung eyes dry and red after a sleepless night. She'd only fallen into a heavy slumber as dawn broke. Last night during the endless hours of darkness, this bed had felt like a torture chamber. This morning she'd pay over her entire fortune to avoid the necessity of ever leaving it.

Her early tea on her nightstand was cold on its tray. She hadn't heard the maid come in, although the girl must have also stayed to stoke the fire blazing merrily in the hearth.

At least something in this room was merry, Sally thought sourly, as she poured cold tea into her cup. She stared at the unappetizing brew, without making any attempt to drink it.

She knew she indulged in a massive attack of self-pity, but that cold tea seemed like an omen for the rest of her life.

A knock at the door, and Caro Nash appeared, bearing another tray. "Good morning, Sally. I'm wondering how you are."

Sally blinked away silly, futile tears, but suspected she wasn't quick enough. "Much better, thank you," she said in a muffled voice. "You didn't have to come up."

Caro gave a dismissive tsk and approached the bed. "I was worried about you last night. Do you still have the headache?"

Yes, but it doesn't compare a jot to the pain in my heart. "It's nothing. But thank you for asking."

"No, don't get up. Breakfast in bed always makes me feel better."

Sally was in no rush to leave her bed, so she

slumped against the pillows as Caro set the loaded tray on her knees. "You're very kind."

"I brought you a couple of rolls and some eggs. But I can ring for bacon and sausages and kidneys, if you'd like those, too."

The thought of cooked meat made Sally's stomach cramp with nausea.

Caro laughed. "Oh, my Lord, you've gone quite green. I'm glad I followed my instincts."

She poured Sally some coffee and passed it to her, then crossed to fling the curtains apart. She turned back in time to catch Sally flinching away from the stark gray light that flooded the room.

Caro grimaced in sympathy. "You do look terrible."

Her friend had a reputation for frankness bordering on tactlessness, and her unconcealed horror as she surveyed Sally made her laugh, despite how miserable she felt. "Thank you very much."

"I'm sorry." Caro had the grace to blush. "Silas is always telling me to think before I speak. But I only remember—"

"After you've spoken?"

"Exactly."

Sally took a sip of coffee. And wished it was hemlock.

If only Morwenna or Amy were here. She liked Caro and Helena, but she didn't feel ready to confide in either of them. Worse, she couldn't bear to become an object of pity—as she would, if these happily married women knew she'd foolishly settled her affections on the man her niece was to wed.

Then she remembered that it was better for everyone if she never revealed her heart's hidden longings. Should Meg ever hear a whisper of Sally's hopeless infatuation, she'd be so upset—and it might create a rift in the family. Easier all round if Sally just suffered in silence.

What a grim prospect.

A concerned expression darkened Caro's deep blue eyes. "I think you should spend the day in bed with a good book. I remember how exhausting the season can be when one is in the thick of things. It's still raining. Nobody will be doing anything exciting today."

Except celebrating Meg's engagement to Sir Charles.

To hide another wince, Sally began to butter one of the crusty rolls, although the thought of food made her gag. It was time to be brave and continue as she meant to go on, no matter what it cost her. She had a lot of practice at that. She summoned the words that murdered all her unworthy hopes.

"No, I'll need to come downstairs to give Sir Charles my approval and congratulate the happy couple—and I'm sure Meg wants to discuss arrangements." She made herself take a bite of her roll.

Caro looked puzzled as she reached for a roll and tore it in half. "What happy couple?"

Sally frowned. "Surely Sir Charles proposed last

night." She took another bite, although the bread tasted like sawdust in her mouth.

Caro bit into her roll and closed her eyes in pleasure. "These are wonderful. Helena's cook is a treasure."

Sally stuck to her guns. "As Meg's aunt, it's my duty to appear."

"Not a bit of it," Caro said cheerfully. "Nobody has proposed to anyone. Or at least not as far as I know."

Sally frowned, her coffee cup halfway to her lips. "But Sir Charles and Meg went off to look at paintings."

"So they did. Are you worried that you're failing as a chaperone?"

"They were alone."

"They were. But Sir Charles is a gentleman, and anyway, Helena hunted them out before too long. No need to worry about scandal compelling a wedding." Caro studied her with sharp eyes. "Or were you hoping that there would be a scandal, and our handsome baronet would have to propose?"

Sally stifled a bleak huff of laughter. If only Caro knew how far she was from the truth. "He's been courting her for weeks. I thought last night he might at last offer for her."

Caro looked surprised. "I didn't realize."

"He's been in constant attendance."

"Yes, but he's always talking to you. Meg's away

chattering about horses with the boys, or talking about dresses with her friends."

"He's only being polite because I'm Meg's aunt."

"Do you think so?" Caro looked unconvinced. "I thought he'd set his sights on you."

Oh, this hurt. It hurt so much. Sally struggled to keep her voice bright, but she clenched her hand, crumbling the roll to pieces. "Don't be silly. I'm too old for him."

Caro's expression didn't lighten. "Rubbish."

"Now you're trying to be tactful."

"Me? Never." Caro's lips quirked with self-deprecating humor. "But if you're positive he's interested in Meg, I suppose you know your business best."

Could her fears be groundless? At least as far as an engagement last night was concerned. Now she thought about it, Sir Charles would be likely to ask her permission before he proposed. "Are you sure they're not engaged?"

Caro took another bite of her roll. "I saw them both at breakfast, and they said not a word about a wedding."

"Perhaps they've decided to wait until Sir Charles has gained my consent."

"Hmm. I still didn't notice any air of conspiracy. If they've agreed to wed, I'm sure I would have picked up something."

Of course she would. It seemed Sally had no need to lurk in her room to avoid news of a betrothal. Pointless to be so relieved. After all, the fact that Sir Charles hadn't proposed last night didn't mean he wouldn't propose later. But Sally swallowed the rest of her coffee and poured another cup, then set to work on her eggs.

"They'll be cold," Caro protested. "Let me ring for some more."

"They're fine," Sally said. She was hungry. She'd barely choked down more than a few mouthfuls of last night's dinner.

Charles was determined to tell Sally that he harbored no romantic interest in her niece. Then he'd move on to proving that he harbored romantic intentions toward her instead.

But as the house party headed toward its end, it seemed Sally was equally set on avoiding his company. He learned to curse the sprawling pile of Shelton Abbey. It was too easy for his quarry to elude him.

Her continuing coldness made him want to snarl. From the first, they'd shared an easy companionship. Now if he entered any room she was in, she found some reason to leave. She could barely endure addressing a few words to him. And when he cornered her into speaking to him, she persisted in addressing the invisible fellow over his right shoulder.

It was all very well for Meg to counsel pouncing.

But a man needed to get within arm's length of the lady before he could take action.

He'd led a fortunate life. Everything he wanted fell to him without undue effort. Born the only son to an adoring family with four older sisters. An assured and extravagant fortune. Clever enough to thrive at school. Strong. Athletic. Cultivated. Confident in society.

The only prize that hadn't tumbled into his hands merely for the asking was the only person important enough to make every other blessing seem insignificant. Damn it all to hell and back.

When he'd decided he wanted Sally Cowan, he'd assumed getting her would be quick and uncomplicated. Now several months into his pursuit, he could almost laugh at his delusions. If he wasn't so devilish unhappy, and thwarted, and bewildered.

And time, which had seemed so plentiful a couple of months ago, became his enemy. The season had only a few weeks left to run. Then as most of the ton did, Sally returned home for the summer.

The house party was at an end. Charles stood with Sally and Meg on Shelton Abbey's front steps, waiting for the carriages to be brought around. West and Helena stood arm in arm behind him, ready to farewell the last of their guests. Caro and Stone and the children had left an hour ago. Brandon and Carey had just ridden away to another house party, a county away in Northamptonshire.

But instead of Sally's carriage rolling into view, her coachman rushed up.

"What is it, Barton?" Sally asked, stepping down to the gravel to meet him. The small group of servants waiting to return to London craned their necks to see what was happening.

"My lady, I'm sorry, but the right front wheel has splintered. Be blowed if I know how it happened. I checked everything last night, and it was right as rain."

"Oh, dear," Sally said in dismay. "How dreadful."

"It will take most of the day to set it right, which means we won't make London tomorrow, even if we get off this afternoon."

"Sally, you're welcome to stay until it's fixed," Helena said.

Meg's annoyed glance at her hostess strengthened Charles's conviction that she'd taken the matter of her aunt's future into her own hands. "But I'm engaged for the Sedgemoors' ball the night we get back, and I do so want to wear my new blue gown."

"If we don't make it, it's not the end of the world," Sally said.

Meg looked sulky. "Everyone's talking about it."

"Then you'll hear all about the ball afterward anyway." Sally sent Meg a quelling glare, then turned to Helena. "Thank you, but you've had your fill of guests this last week."

"Not at all," Helena said.

West smiled at Sally. "You're no trouble."

Meg shot Charles a meaningful look, confirming his suspicion that the broken wheel was no accident. A long trip back to London? Sally couldn't avoid him if they were on the road together, and he'd be on the lookout for his chance to get her alone.

He seized his moment and stepped down to stand beside Sally. "Why don't you both come with me? I'd appreciate the company. That way, your coachman can make his repairs and leave when he's ready."

Meg's "Oh, how delightful that would be," clashed with Sally's "We couldn't put you to such trouble."

"It would be my pleasure," Charles said smoothly.

When Sally turned pale, he moved to catch her arm. For a sizzling moment, he touched her. How could she be so cold to him when she felt so warm?

After these last frustrating days, his patience with her skittishness was rapidly running out. It was time she understood what he wanted of her. Somewhere on this trip, he'd say his piece, and if she sent him away, at least he'd know where he stood.

"How kind of you to offer, Sir Charles," Helena said, with a glint in her eye that hinted she was awake to Meg's strategems and meant to promote them.

"Helena, you said it would be all right to stay until the repair is made," Sally said with a desperation that made Charles grit his teeth.

"Of course you're welcome, but what a pity for Meg to miss the Sedgemoor ball," Helena said. "It promises to be the highlight of the season."

"Aunt, please?" Meg looked as deprived as a pretty girl wearing a traveling dress in the first stare of fashion could manage.

"It would be no inconvenience, Lady Norwood," Charles said. Unwilling admiration at Meg's cheek vied with curiosity about what she planned.

"Aunt, it makes the most sense," Meg said. "What can possibly be your objection?"

With a hunted expression, Sally pulled out of his hold. On the verge of victory, Charles found it in himself to feel sorry for her. Because what could she say?

He watched her square her shoulders as if preparing for an ordeal. Had he really fallen so low in her esteem? Or was Meg right that this jumpiness was a good sign? These last days, he'd had plenty of time to contemplate her behavior. If she found him attractive, but was muddle-headed enough to believe he'd chosen Meg, she had every cause to eschew his company.

He hoped to hell that wasn't wishful thinking.

"Oh, I'm silly to hesitate." She summoned a gallant smile for that invisible cove behind him. "Thank you, Sir Charles. I appreciate your kind offer, and I'll gratefully accept."

"Capital," he said with a composure that in no way expressed the jubilation in his heart.

As Sally started to give orders to Barton and her other servants, Charles caught Meg's eye. He hid a smile when she gave him a surreptitious wink.

CHAPTER EIGHT

*S*ally would rather have all her teeth removed with pliers than spend two days on the road, struggling to hide her feelings from Sir Charles.

Curse that broken wheel, however it had occurred. She hadn't had her carriage out in the week since she'd arrived, so it must have been damaged on the drive to Shelton Abbey. Which was odd in itself. Barton always did a thorough check on the vehicle once it reached its destination.

As they covered the miles to London, the day was beautiful and fragrant with late spring. A luggage coach followed with Sir Charles's valet and Meg and Sally's maids, but it couldn't hope to keep up with a natty yellow and black curricle built for speed.

To save them all being squashed onto one seat in the open carriage, Sir Charles rode his gray horse beside them, while Meg took the reins. Heavens, he must be in love with the girl, to trust her with his high-strung horses. Sally almost wished he'd hurry up and propose to her niece. This was like waiting for the ax to fall.

Meg was so busy driving that she didn't try to engage Sally in conversation. Which was a huge relief. Even if her silence left Sally's mind too free to gnaw over the insuperable problem of falling in love with the wrong man.

Over the last days, she'd tried telling herself that she suffered from a passing madness. But so far, while it was definitely a madness, it showed no signs of passing. Since that agonizing moment when she'd heard Sir Charles declare his intentions to marry another woman, she'd done her best to belittle her feelings, to crush them to nothing.

To no avail.

Nor had she been prepared for her physical reaction to his presence, now she'd acknowledged her love. The merest sight of him, even in the distance, set her heart racing like one of West's champion thoroughbreds. She felt hot and cold, and tingly and lightheaded. This wicked, rapacious desire was a fever eating her up from inside.

No woman of her mature years should be struck dumb at the sight of a handsome man. But when Sir Charles was near, her hands itched to explore that tall, powerful body. She trembled with forbidden excitement, and her stomach churned with unacceptable impulses. The sound of his deep voice made every nerve tighten with longing.

She'd become so terrified of someone noticing her turmoil that she'd done her best to avoid Sir Charles's company. But being away from him didn't calm the raging storm of need inside her.

She bit back a groan, fortunately muffled by the rattle of the wheels and the creak of the harness. When he married Meg, Sally would have to present a joyful face to the world. She owed it to her niece. Heavens, she owed it to herself. She had some pride.

Now she faced the awful prospect of a future where Meg and Sir Charles joined in family events. And all the time, Sally would have to pretend that he meant nothing more to her than her niece's husband.

Most of Sir Charles's lands were in the west, in Shropshire. There was some small consolation in that. Sally lived on the estate outside Portsmouth that had been set aside as her widow's portion. With Meg blissfully ensconced on the Welsh borders and Sally licking her wounds in the south, at least she wouldn't often see the couple.

That should make her feel better. But her traitorous heart ached at the idea of him so far away, even if he was married to another woman.

Curse this love. There was no logic to it. Just pointless suffering.

Perhaps she should consider retiring to a convent. Or emigrating.

No, she wasn't going to run away. Her yen for Charles Kinglake would not conquer her. She would master this weakness.

But not today...

Her gaze strayed to where he rode ahead. With no risk of him seeing her yearning and with Meg concentrating on the road, she yielded to the dangerous temptation to stare her fill. Even as she knew it was fatal to feed her appetite, she couldn't help thrilling to what a magnificent sight he presented.

He rode as if born to the saddle, with the easy, unflashy competence he devoted to everything in his life. His hat perched at a jaunty angle on his thick coffee-brown hair. The shoulders in the exquisitely cut blue coat were straight and strong.

Her hand clenched on the side of the carriage, and she blinked back tears, despite this morning's strictures to herself to waste no more time crying over this mess.

After several hours, Sir Charles drew back to ride beside the carriage. "I've arranged to change the team at the next inn. We can stop for a meal, too."

Sally bent her head, hoping her bonnet hid her strained expression. "Excellent."

"I'll also send a boy ahead to engage some rooms for you tonight at the Angel in Woburn. It's a fine hostelry, and I've already reserved a bed for myself."

"You're very kind," Sally said after a pause, wondering what the devil was wrong with Meg. The privilege of handling these superb horses seemed to have left her speechless.

"Not at all," he said, and urged his horse to a fast canter that took him ahead once more.

At the coaching inn, Sir Charles arranged for a cold collation to be served in a private parlor. Sally picked at her meal, while he and Meg discussed the finer points of driving his pair.

He'd stabled a change of horses here for the return journey, and Meg was voluble in her excitement about trying them, too. Whatever had kept her silent must no longer matter. Sally hardly paid attention, until she heard Sir Charles mention her name.

"I think Lady Norwood wants to return to London as soon as possible."

"It wouldn't be much of a detour," Meg said, in the voice she used when she intended to coax someone into giving her her way. It was a tone Sally had become familiar with in the last few months. Meg was generally a good girl, but by heaven, she knew what she wanted.

"What wouldn't?" Sally raised her head and wondered what she'd missed.

"My friend Perdita Gailes lives near here. When I wrote to tell her about Lord West's house party and who was invited, she said Sir Charles has a hunting box just off the main road. I'd love to see it."

Sally frowned. "I thought you wanted to get back for the Sedgemoor ball."

"I do. But we made excellent time this morning, and the hunting box is only a few miles out of our way. Isn't that right, Sir Charles?"

"Down some very winding lanes. And it's all shut up. I haven't even got any staff in the place, apart from the gamekeeper and his wife. I only use it for the autumn hunting."

With his attention on Meg, Sally stole a chance to admire his fine profile and the set of his shoulders. Honestly she was her own worst enemy. Under the table, her hands curled against her skirts as she fought the forbidden urge to touch him.

"I hear the countryside is beautiful." Meg sent him a meaningful look that Sally couldn't interpret. "Please, Sir Charles."

Sir Charles arched his eyebrows as if questioning Meg's silent demand. Even through her preoccupation, Sally's curiosity stirred. Her companions seemed to be conducting another conversation, separate from the spoken one.

Had they reached an understanding before they left Shelton Abbey? Despite wanting this horrible suspense to end, the thought twisted her stomach into an agonizing knot.

"As long as your aunt doesn't mind." He glanced at Sally and caught her gaze before she hurriedly looked away. Her hunger was so powerful and new, she feared he'd see it burning like fire in her eyes.

She dredged up a smile for Meg. "As you're so agog to see the property, of course we'll go, mousekin. But if it means we're late into London and you miss the ball, I don't want to hear a word about it."

Meg leaped up to hug Sally. "Thank you, Aunt. You're such a good sport."

Meg's open affection threatened to shatter Sally's barely maintained control. Briefly she returned the girl's embrace, then disentangled herself.

She felt so guilty about the jealousy eating at her. It wasn't Meg's fault that she was Sir Charles's choice.

He watched them both with a speculative expression, then he stood with sudden purpose. "If we're going, there's no time to be lost."

Charles dismounted outside his gamekeeper's cottage at the gates of the isolated estate. Meg pulled the new team to a stop on the drive a few feet away.

Miss Meg proved to be a fine whip. And a skilled schemer.

Charles had no doubt she was responsible for today's circumstances. That wheel of Sally's carriage had been broken a little too conveniently. And he was sure she had plans in place for this visit to his obscure and rather neglected hunting box.

Did she intend to make herself scarce so he could initiate the pounce strategy?

He buzzed with excitement at the thought. Sally hadn't warmed up over the miles since they'd left Shelton Abbey, he regretted to say. So right now, he was inclined to play along with Meg.

He knocked on the door, surprised when the noise didn't set the dogs barking. The door opened to Mrs. Brown, his gamekeeper's wife, dressed in a bonnet and gloves, and obviously on her way out.

"Sir Charles," she said in a flutter. She glanced at Meg and Sally and managed a hurried curtsy. "Your ladyships."

"Mrs. Brown, I apologize for not letting you know I was coming."

"Do you need the house opened up?"

"No, it's only a brief call. If Brown could unlock the door, we'll do our tour, then be on our way."

"Brown's not here, sir. He's gone over to Squire Harlow to get some pheasant chicks. He won't be back until tomorrow."

"I'll just take the key, then. No need to worry yourself. I can see you're on an errand."

Nervously she touched her straw bonnet. Behind her, he saw two laden baskets and a small trunk. "My sister in Harborough isn't well. She had a bairn last week, and she's poorly after it. I'm off to run the house for her while she gets back on her feet."

Harborough was a good thirty miles away. Mrs.

Brown would be lucky to get there by nightfall, even if she left this minute. "Then you must go to her."

"Oh, you are kind, Sir Charles. I can wait a few minutes and put a luncheon together for you, although I fear it will be plain fare."

He shook his head. "We've eaten, thank you. You go ahead and never mind us. I'll be back for the hunting in August."

"Thank you, sir," she said with another curtsy.

"The key?"

"Oh, dear, my head is all over the place today." She disappeared into a room off the hallway and reappeared with a heavy iron key. "All should be in order. I went through and did a good clean at the start of the week."

"Thank you, Mrs. Brown." He accepted the key. "Let me know how your sister fares."

He remounted and turned his horse down the long, winding drive to the house. Behind him, Meg clicked her tongue to the horses to get them moving. Sally remained silent. She'd been quiet for the whole trip. So much for his hopes that his company on the road might melt the ice between them.

They traveled through thick woods and emerged onto a graveled forecourt. Before them stood a delightful doll's house of a building, red brick, three stories high, with tall windows and a steeply raked, tiled roof. Although he rarely visited, Charles had always been fond of this lovely little house, lost dreaming in its deep woods.

"This is lovely," Sally said, taking in the charming view.

For once she spoke without prompting, even if she still didn't look at him. He stopped his horse beside the carriage and smiled. "My father built it for my mother. I call it a hunting box, and that's what I mostly use it for. But I have a feeling Papa intended it as a place to escape the children."

"How romantic." Sally's voice was warmer than it had been in days. Whatever Meg was plotting, so far it seemed to be working. "I had a feeling you came from a happy family."

What a turn up. Sally showed some interest in him. His hopes ratcheted another notch higher. "Yes, I was lucky. Parents who doted on each other and on their five children. Four older sisters who adored their little brother. You're lucky I'm not completely insufferable."

To his delight, Sally laughed. It sounded rusty, but he wasn't fussy. This was the closest they'd come in days to their old amity. "But of course modesty is one of your many perfections."

He made an ironic bow in her direction. "Indeed it is."

"Will you please show us through the house, Sir Charles?" Meg set the brake as he dismounted and tied his horse to the back of the carriage.

"It would be my pleasure." He stepped over to help Sally alight.

By now he should be accustomed to the zap of response when he touched her, even through the decorous layers of their gloves. Her fingers trembled, and for a fleeting moment when her green eyes met his, he wondered if his case mightn't be lost after all. His fingers tightened, and it took an effort to release her and help Meg down.

"My friend was right about the fine countryside, and this is such a pretty house." Meg's hand didn't linger in his, and she ascended the flight of shallow steps toward the tall front door.

Sally lingered behind, looking around at the woods that encircled the clearing. There were no formal gardens around the house. Up to where the trees began, lawn scattered with wildflowers surrounded the building.

"It's like something out of a fairytale. The Beast's estate or Sleeping Beauty's castle. I'm so glad you brought us here."

A dreamy smile curved her lips. Damn it, he'd give up his hope of heaven if she looked at him like that.

"So am I," Charles said fervently.

Her expression closed, and she cast him a wary glance. Blast. Sally might have gone back to speaking to him, but he needed to step carefully.

When he strode up to the door, the key turned with ease. The Browns were scrupulous caretakers. There were no creaky doors on this estate. The minute he stepped into the hall, behind the ladies, he smelled beeswax and lavender.

In the dimness, Sally and Meg were mere shadows, until he flung open the shutters to reveal a graceful hall with paneled walls and black and white floor tiles. Light flooded in to illuminate Sally in her dark green traveling dress. His heart turned a somersault and his breath caught. She was such a lovely woman. Surely fate couldn't be so cruel as to bring this glorious creature into his orbit, then keep him from possessing her.

He sucked in his first full breath in what felt like days. Things headed in the direction he wanted. Right now, she looked much more like the vivacious lady he remembered from London. Her vivid face was alight with interest and pleasure as she looked around her.

"Does the house have a name?" Sally stood next to him and looked through the window at the pretty view.

Would wonders never cease? The last few days, she'd run a mile every time he'd ventured near her.

When Charles caught the drift of her evocative scent, desire stirred hard and urgent. But it was too soon to make his move. And he needed to get rid of Meg.

He shifted back to take off his hat and set it on a chair. "My father called it *Sans Souci.*"

"'Without care?' How apt. It's as if the world and its troubles are a thousand miles away."

He felt like cheering. The distance she'd established

between them narrowed by the minute. The instant he'd met her, he'd felt an immediate affinity, as though he could tell her anything and she'd understand. He wanted her as a man wanted a woman he desired. But he also valued their friendship. The recent chill between them had oppressed his soul.

"I'm so glad you like it," he said, smiling and wishing he could kiss her this very moment. As she straightened and surveyed the room with wide green eyes, she looked like she needed kissing. "Meg, I'm grateful you suggested this detour."

No answer.

He turned. When he and Sally had entered the house, Meg had lingered beside the door. There was no sign of her now.

"Where is Meg?" Sally asked.

"She's probably checking the horses." Charles barely avoided rubbing his hands together in satisfaction. "You know she can't stay away from them."

Sally frowned, and he had a second to regret that everyday matters pierced her sweet wonder. "I'll just make sure."

"She won't go far. She said she wanted to see something of the estate." As far as he was concerned, the girl could walk the entire boundary, as long as she left him alone with Sally.

"Let me check."

After she went outside, he heard a sharp exclamation of displeasure. "What on earth are you doing?"

The outrage in Sally's voice had Charles rushing outside. Meg was perched in his carriage's driving seat with a daredevil expression on her face.

"I can't come so close to Perdita without going to see her," she called, setting the carriage in motion. "I'll only be a couple of hours."

"Wait," Sally cried, running down the steps after her, but Meg had already urged the horses to a canter. "Meg, stop!"

Despite his self-interest, Sally's frantic tone spurred him into pursuit. He sprinted across the gravel to catch the girl, but she had too much of a start on him.

"Meg, damn well come back here," Charles shouted. By the time he stopped, gasping, well down the drive, she was out of sight.

"Damned brat," he muttered, even though nobody was there to hear him.

He and Sally were marooned. The chit had been deuced clever, and circumstances had favored her plans. The Browns were the only people who lived within easy reach, and they were both absent from home. Brown wouldn't be back until late tomorrow, and Mrs. Brown would be away until her sister was well again. Charles had even tied his horse to the back of the carriage to make it easy for Meg to leave her aunt stranded with him.

He'd wanted to be alone with Sally, but this smacked too much of a conspiracy. God knows what Sally thought was going on.

Damn it, if she suspected he was a party to the scheme, the small steps he'd made back into her favor today would mean nothing.

He sucked in a breath and jogged back toward the house. He hoped to hell Meg did mean to return some time this afternoon. Much as he longed to make Sally his wife, he wanted her to choose him freely. He didn't want her niece's recklessness to spark a scandal that forced her into an uncongenial marriage.

Another uncongenial marriage.

Still, all wasn't lost. He and Sally were alone at last. For a couple of hours. If he read her right, she was in a more receptive frame of mind than recently. And he had half a dozen bedrooms at his disposal.

By God, it was time to take charge and show Sally just how much he wanted her. And if heaven stayed on his side, she'd finally admit that she wanted him, too.

Anticipation thrummed in his blood like a drum beat. Although given his lack of success so far, he might be over-optimistic about how this might play out.

Whatever happened, he couldn't ignore this chance. He just had to trust that fortune favored the brave.

CHAPTER NINE

*S*hocked and outraged, Sally waited on the steps for Sir Charles to return from what was sure to be a futile pursuit. She'd seen Meg's determined expression as she drove away, and she was under no illusions that her niece intended to be caught.

What had got into the girl? And what did she expect this ridiculous prank to achieve? Was this a ploy to leave her alone with Sir Charles, so he could obtain Sally's permission to seek Meg's hand? It seemed a bizarre way to ensure an interview.

"She outran me," Sir Charles called as he came out of the trees.

"I could strangle her," Sally said, too angry to pretend that this was a minor escapade. "What on earth is her game?"

Sir Charles crossed the forecourt and ran up the

steps toward her, his smile wry. "I think she wants to give us a chance to talk."

Oh, no. Perhaps he was about to ask her permission to marry her niece. Sally would have to say yes, but it would feel like drinking acid.

She regarded him warily. "We talk all the time."

He grimaced. "Not lately. You've done your best to avoid me over the last few days."

"Oh." She'd hoped he wouldn't notice.

When he took her arm, she jumped like a startled rabbit. She told herself to pull away, but the warmth flooding her veins was too delicious.

Dear Lord, she was a disaster. How could she hope to scotch this infatuation if she stole every opportunity to nourish it?

"Come inside," Sir Charles said, his deep voice steady. "There's no point staring after her. She won't come back until she's ready."

How she appreciated his equable temper. Many men, her late husband included, would rage and curse at Meg's foolishness. And probably end up blaming Sally for their predicament.

"She's usually such a biddable girl." Sally said, not entirely honestly.

"When it suits her, I suspect," Sir Charles responded wryly. "Miss Meg and I understand each other very well."

What exactly did that mean? Did understanding Meg mean they had an understanding? Sally was too much of a coward to ask. "When she comes back, I'll speak sternly to her."

"I doubt it will do much good. She's a headstrong creature in her self-effacing way." Sir Charles kept hold of Sally's arm and drew her back inside the house. "Although I'm sure you'll feel better if you read her a lecture."

"Should we ask Mrs. Brown for help?" Sally struggled to control a pang of disappointment when he released her and wandered over to stare out the window.

"She's going to her sister's. We caught her on the way out. And Mr. Brown is twenty miles away."

Oh, dear, it sounded like they were stuck here. Trepidation trickled down Sally's spine. It had been hard enough hiding her yen for Sir Charles in a crowd of people. Here where they were alone, she had a sick feeling that he'd discover she felt much more than friendship for him.

And that promised years of awkward family gatherings, once he'd married Meg.

Her hands unsteady, Sally took off her bonnet and set it on a carved Jacobean chest against the wall. "Is there a village nearby?"

"No. I warned you both that the property is isolated. The nearest village is Upton, but it's a good ten miles away."

"Anyway," she said, striving to be sensible as she stripped off her gloves, "we need to stay here and wait for

Meg to come back. There's no point in us getting lost, too. Do you know how far the Gailes estate is from here?"

"Seven miles at least." He turned to her. "If you wish, I can go cross-country to find it. Or try to make it to Upton."

Sally shook her head. "What would that achieve?"

"We're alone in this house. I don't want you to feel unsafe." He moved behind her to help her take off her pelisse. When he leaned close enough for her to catch the clean scent of his skin, her ungovernable heart missed a beat.

"I trust you," she mumbled, trying to steady her breath.

Of course she trusted him. He wasn't interested in her.

"Thank you. I appreciate that." To her astonishment, he placed his hands on her shoulders and gave them an encouraging squeeze. "But you must know if word gets out about this, it will damage your reputation."

She made a dismissive sound and turned to face him, dislodging his hold. But the heat of his touch still sizzled through her veins and whispered temptation. "I'm a widow of advanced years and unsullied reputation. Nobody is going to question our actions."

"Devil take you, Sally." He frowned as he tugged off his gloves and shoved them in his pocket. "I wish you wouldn't do that."

"Do what?" She'd forgotten that it was dangerous to

look into his face. He was close enough for her to see all the varied shades of brown in his eyes. And the thick black lashes shadowing them.

For one lost moment, she swayed toward him, before sense asserted itself and she stepped away. Her knees felt horridly shaky.

"Talk about yourself as if you were too old for scandal. You're a lovely, sparkling woman and, believe me, if society finds out I had you to myself, the male half of the ton will be green with envy."

She started to laugh, but something in his expression quashed her amusement. "Sir Charles, I think you mean that," she said in surprise.

A muscle flickered in his cheek, and those toffee eyes focused somber and intent upon her face. "I've never meant anything more."

"You're so kind," she said wonderingly, suffering once again that powerful urge to lean into him.

He caught her hand. The shock of his bare skin on hers shuddered through her like a lightning strike. "No, damn it, I'm not being kind."

She wanted to argue, but couldn't summon the words. Having spent days avoiding the penetrating dark gaze, she stared up into his chiseled features and couldn't look away even if an earthquake struck.

"What have I done to offend you?" His grip on her hand tightened, and his expression turned urgent. "Lately you've barely given me the time of day. Whatever it is, let me make it up to you. I hate it when you're cold to me."

Somewhere at the back of her mind, a voice screamed that he shouldn't care, that she played no important role in his life. But that piercing gaze held her captive. And her awakening desire nailed her feet to the floor.

It was intoxicating to have this marvelous man staring down at her, as if nothing else in the world existed.

"You haven't offended me. How could you?" She licked dry lips and watched his eyes flicker down to the betraying movement. With a desperate attempt to return to something like their usual interactions, she said, "I don't think you should be holding my hand."

He didn't let her go. "I like it."

"So do I," she admitted, before she questioned the prudence of honesty.

"Sally—"

"And I don't think you should call me Sally."

"For God's sake, call me Charles."

Urgency roughened his deep baritone and made her shiver with longing. She'd been so wise to avoid his gaze. Now that she stared up at him, she couldn't stop.

She'd never before realized how many shades of brown there were in the world. Honey. Russet. Deep, dark brown. Burnt caramel. Gazing into Sir Charles's eyes, she felt like she drowned in hot treacle. What a splendid path to oblivion.

Her hand trembled in his, but she still couldn't summon the will to withdraw, when this might be her only chance to touch him. Her heart beat high and frantic in her throat.

It was like being utterly terrified. Except somehow she wasn't.

She made a halfhearted effort to pull away, but didn't get anywhere. "We're alone here."

His lips flattened. "Believe me, I know."

"We should...we should try and remember the proprieties."

"Why?"

She made herself blink, but still everything in this room except Sir Charles's powerful form receded into unreality. She felt dizzy, and her unreliable knees threatened to collapse beneath her. Her grip on his fingers firmed, and she told herself, without believing a word of it, that she only held onto him because she was afraid of falling.

"Because..."

Heaven help her, she couldn't think of a single reason. She fell back on repeating herself and knew in doing so, she lost the argument. "Because we're alone."

His gaze sparked with the humor she'd noticed and liked from the first. Those fascinating lines around his eyes deepened. "All the more reason to seize my chance."

Had he edged nearer? The heat radiating from his large, masculine body made every hair on her skin stand up. A hot, heavy weight started to throb in the pit of her stomach. Her breath jammed in her throat, making her even more lightheaded.

Heaven help her, she'd never felt like this before.

"I think…I think I need to sit down. I'm not feeling at all well," she said faintly.

"Let me help you. You're looking a little flushed."

She quivered with wanton delight as a powerful male arm curled around her waist.

"Sir Charles…" She tried to make his name sound like a protest, but even in her own ears, it emerged like a sigh of surrender.

"Charles."

She placed her hands flat on his chest and tried to ignore how broad and hard he was under her palms, like sun-warmed rock. "You should let me go."

"Never."

"This isn't right," she whispered. Her tight throat made speech almost impossible.

Surely that couldn't be desire in his eyes. If she'd come to terms with one thing during these last days, it was that he couldn't possibly want her.

"It feels right to me. Doesn't it feel right to you?"

"I…" She struggled to lie and say it didn't. But the woeful truth was that she loved being this close to him. She loved the drift of his warm, musky scent, and the pressure of his large, capable hand against the small of her back. Especially when she'd never imagined he'd touch her like this. "I can't see this as proper behavior."

Had he moved closer still? "I'm not doing anything that I haven't done when we've danced."

"In a room full of people." That large, capable hand firmed, curving her toward him.

It would be so easy to succumb. She wanted him so much. In a final, desperate attempt to wrench herself back to bitter reality, she forced herself to mention the forbidden topic. "What about Meg?"

His grip tightened on her waist, and hard as she tried, she could find no trace of guilt in his face. "To hell with Meg."

"What?" she stammered.

"What about us?"

She told herself to resist the press of his hand, but she felt her bones softening in surrender. "There is no us."

"You don't mean that."

The awful truth was she didn't. She battled to muster further protest. The mention of her niece should have brought this always gentlemanly gentleman back to his senses, but his eyes only burned hotter as he surveyed her.

"I…"

"You say you trust me, Sally."

"Of course I do," she said quickly, even though right now she wasn't sure that was true. "And don't call me Sally."

He gave a soft huff of laughter. "I can't call a woman I've kissed Lady Norwood."

"Ki…" She gulped for air and told herself to put this impudent fellow in his place. "But you haven't."

"I'm getting ahead of myself." His other large hand cupped the back of her head. Heat sizzled through her, stole what little air remained in her lungs. "You must forgive me."

Why the devil didn't her legs work? One might almost imagine she stood here and agreed to let Sir Charles kiss her. "I won't forgive you if you kiss me," she whispered.

She saw he didn't believe her denials. Why would he? She certainly didn't. The shameful truth was that if he didn't kiss her in the next second, she'd shatter into a million pieces.

"It will be worth it." His face was now so near that his breath whispered across her lips like a promise of the kiss to come.

The teasing delay was torture. She forgot everything except her need to feel that clever, sensual mouth on hers. Even if she was damned for it.

She couldn't contain a choked sound of yearning.

Of course he heard the incoherent desire in the whimper. His brown gaze flared gold, then her eyes fluttered closed as his lips touched hers. With a sigh, she arched into him and parted her lips.

His mouth was hard and purposeful, and the masterful contact shook her to the soles of her feet. She'd expected gentleness because he was a kind, considerate man, a civilized man. But he kissed her as if he wanted to devour her.

Sally made a muffled sound of astonished delight and kissed him back with every ounce of secret longing in her heart.

His arms lashed around her, crushing her to him. When she'd stared into his eyes, she thought she'd come close to drowning. She'd had no idea. A towering wave of sensual enjoyment overwhelmed her, destroyed all capacity for thought, banished fear of scandal, made her a slave to her clamoring senses.

His hands moved up and down her back, and he tugged her against him so she felt the hammer blows of his heartbeat. She also became aware of his blatant arousal.

His unabashed desire excited her, fed her own desire. Shamelessly, she pressed into him. On a surge of excitement, she dug her fingers into his head to deepen his kiss.

She couldn't bear for this to end. She couldn't bear to go back to being lonely and unwanted.

Charles wanted her. She could have no doubt of that. His tongue swept into her mouth, making her moan in welcome. The next time he did that, she tentatively met him, fluttering her tongue against his.

He groaned and gathered her higher, cradling her between his thighs, making no secret of his need. Her core ached for that hard weight to fill her, pound into her, claim her as his.

With a groan, he staggered forward until her back hit the wall. She gasped into his mouth, and he raised his head to look at her.

Perhaps even then, if she hadn't met his eyes, she might have doused the conflagration building between them. If she'd seen a trace of triumph in his face, she'd have found the strength to pull back.

But what she read in his expression sliced straight to her yearning heart. He looked tender and desperate and eager.

She knew he asked her a question. However silently. A question that flew in the face of her duty, and her virtue, and all her plans for the future.

Staring up into his face, her only answer could be yes.

She summoned a shaky smile and ran one hand from his shoulder to where his heart thundered with desire for her. "Charles…"

When he heard her say his name, his lips curved in an answering smile that brought out those beguiling dimples. He touched her cheek with a tenderness that matched the tenderness in his eyes.

This time, in his kiss, she felt reverence as well as hunger. Sally's husband, the only other man to touch her carnally, had never treated her as if she were anything special. Charles was shaking with need. The last vestiges of her resistance melted away to nothing.

When Charles stroked her breast, she made a husky sound of encouragement.

"Lovely." His thumb flicked a nipple beaded with arousal.

A searing thrill ripped through her and stoked that restless, heavy feeling between her legs. "Yes, lovely," she sighed.

Charles placed his other hand on the wall near her head and kissed her again. This time his kiss was sweet. At least at first.

Soon she was clinging to him and sucking his tongue deep into her mouth. He tasted like heaven. Male and powerful and hot. She ran her fingers through his thick brown hair and gave it a subtle pull to tell him not to stop. When he squeezed her breast, she cried out.

Abruptly he raised his head and tugged her away from the wall. With an easy strength that made her heart cartwheel, he swung her up into his arms and carried her through to the next room where a chaise longue stood near the unlit fire.

Sally sucked in a quivery breath as he laid her down. She tried to tell herself they'd gone far enough. She should stop him now before they did anything irrevocable.

But as she saw him standing over her in the shadows, she couldn't gather the words to banish this spell that held them captive. She'd never felt so alive as she did when Charles kissed her. The thought of returning to her cold, lonely life made her stomach cramp in horrified denial. Nobody there kissed her as if it was a matter of life and death.

She might never have another chance to experience pleasure, to give herself to the man she wanted above all others. It asked too much of a mere mortal to reject the exquisite gift of his passion.

Right now, this magnificent man wanted her. She meant to have him, whatever it cost her.

She sat up against the arm of the chaise and stretched out her hand. "Come to me, Charles."

CHAPTER TEN

*E*ven through the rush of rising excitement, Charles knew he should question this sudden capitulation, this quick switch from distance to desire. He should slow down, declare his intentions, inquire after Sally's, gain some commitment that her consent meant to her what it meant to him.

But he'd spent endless weeks longing for her, separated from her by a pane of glass he couldn't shatter. To have her with him now, warm, welcoming, willing, how the devil could he pause and take stock before proceeding?

"Oh, my darling," he breathed, flinging off his coat and seizing her hand. He brought it to his lips and covered it with kisses, all the time watching desire turned her green eyes to dark jade. Even through the dim light, he read the naked demand in her expression.

Setting one knee on the chaise longue, he straddled

her. He slid his arms around her back and brought her up for another kiss. He couldn't get enough of that luscious mouth, of her tangy flavor. She curled her arms around his neck and responded with the readiness that had shocked him at first and still filled him with surprised gratitude.

The hint of inexperience in her kisses touched his heart, reminded him to cherish her. One day, she'd tell him about her marriage, but now he knew enough to understand that she needed his care as well as his ardor.

"I want you so much," she murmured, trailing her lips along the side of his face. "Don't make me wait."

"Sally…"

"Please."

He kissed her neck, delighting in how she trembled. Nor was he much steadier. His shaking hands took forever to loosen the lacing at the back of her green dress.

Gently he slid her bodice down to reveal her beautiful breasts. At the sight of her pearled pink nipples, need jolted him like a sharp blow to the belly.

"Oh," she squeaked and raised her hands to cover herself.

"Let me see," he said in a choked voice.

For a moment, she hesitated, then slowly she lay back and lowered her hands. With a pride that made his heart crack, she raised her chin.

"Perfect," he whispered, and stroked and squeezed until she squirmed with longing.

When he took one pebbled nipple between his lips and flicked his tongue across it, she cried out and buried her hand in his hair. The rhythm her fingertips set up against his scalp matched the ravenous beat of his blood.

Dear God above, he had to have her.

He slid his hand under her skirts and found her skin. Warm. Smooth. He pushed the loose drawers up until he could slip his hand between her legs, stroking her through the frail lawn. She was wet and aroused. After doubting that she wanted him at all, he loved that she couldn't hide her swift response. The heady scent of her arousal threatened to send him mad.

With sudden ruthlessness, he rose and knelt between her legs. He shoved up her skirts and reached down to rip her drawers, revealing her to his avid eyes. Light brown curls, glistening with proof of her need. The pale plain of her stomach with its sweet little navel.

She was slender and graceful with long dancer's legs. His imagination hadn't come close to picturing how beautiful she was under her clothes.

Unable to resist temptation, he bowed his head and tilted her hips. He buried his mouth in that satiny cleft, tasting her intimately and finding her sweeter than honey.

She stiffened and gasped in shock, but he soon had her sighing and undulating against him. When he worked his tongue against her center, she gave a cracked cry and grasped his shoulders. She quivered against his seeking mouth before on another cry, she reached her climax. He lapped at her as she floated down from the heights, then raised his head to stare into her face.

Sally was flushed, and her features were soft with the aftermath of pleasure. But he couldn't mistake the surprise in her eyes.

"What…what was that?"

Hell, what a damned clumsy brute her husband must have been.

As Charles smiled, her salty taste was rich on his tongue. "You liked it?"

"It made me feel wicked." Her voice was husky.

"But you liked it?"

Her blush intensified. "You know I did."

"Good." He placed a kiss on one satiny white thigh. Then he sat up to unbutton his breeches. As his heart raced with rapacious anticipation, he fumbled with the uncooperative fastenings.

The moment he saw her, he'd wanted her, come to love her not long after that. She'd put him through hell since. Having her sprawled before him, panting as she quivered after her first climax, beggared his wildest dreams.

Her passion-darkened gaze settled where his cock

stood out from his breeches. "Dear Lord above," she whispered and lifted her hand.

He braced for her caress, but shyness caught her at the last moment.

"Touch me," Charles grated out, catching her hand and placing it on him.

Heat from the contact blasted through him and threatened his precarious control. He clenched his teeth and fought the urge to lose himself in her hand.

Her fingers trembled under his, but he saw fascination in her face, as she instinctively curled into a fist around him.

Another thundering shudder of heat. He closed his eyes as she tentatively shifted up toward the sensitive tip.

"Am I…am I hurting you?" she asked unsteadily, stroking down again. Thank God, without releasing him.

"No." Speaking was damned difficult when the fireworks shooting through his head were fit to rival the damned Battle of Waterloo. "Harder."

She firmed her grip and moved her hand, finding her own rhythm after a few false starts that nearly took the top of his head off. Her unskilled caresses threatened to incinerate him to smoking shards.

He caught her spread thighs as if clinging to a precipice, and let her have her way. The pleasure verged on unbearable torment. It would be so easy—

safer—to spill into her fist. But this first time, there was no way in Hades he'd miss being inside her.

When she brushed her thumb across the damp head, he reached the limit of his restraint. Roughly he snatched at her hand, but the kiss he placed on her knuckles was gentle. Her skin had caught his musk. "I can't wait a second longer."

Sally's eyes deepened, and her lips parted. "Charles…"

"I love to hear you say my name." He leaned in and kissed her with open-mouthed hunger. She hooked her hands over his shoulders and fitted her body to his.

He ripped at his neck cloth, flinging it to the floor. A low sound of feminine approval emerged from her throat. With greedy hands, she pushed aside his shirt, and he groaned as her palms flattened over the bare skin of his chest.

When she placed a kiss between his nipples, the sweetness squeezed his heart. He twined his hand in her tumble of hair and held her still for another voracious kiss.

With his other hand, he stroked her, reveling in her liquid response. The scent of arousal thickening the air teased him with the promise of looming fulfillment.

"Oh, that's good," Sally sighed, angling toward his caresses.

When she curled her arms across his back, pulling him down to her, he could delay no longer. Rising on one arm so he could watch every second of this transcendent consummation, he pressed into her.

He met slippery heat and glorious resistance. Then with a deep groan of triumph, he slid into her as if they were born to join together.

She released a surprised gasp and tightened around him. The sensation threatened his threadbare control, but he tensed every muscle against release.

He meant above all to pleasure her. Magnificent as this union was for him, he burned to show Sally what heights a woman could reach with a skilled and considerate lover.

He met her eyes, glassy like the ocean on a sultry summer day. Then on a hard kiss, he shifted deeper. She gave a faint, broken cry and arched into him. Her fingers dug into the muscles of his back, as if the world reeled for her, too.

Blindness descended on Charles, and he hurtled into an inferno of unfettered passion. Gripped by purely animal instinct, he withdrew. Then he pushed forward, claiming her again and luxuriating in the grip of her body.

On a husky moan, she raised her knees higher, changing the angle. He shifted to meet her and felt her open in marvelous welcome. She shoved up his shirt, so her fingernails scored his back. The sting added to the riot of sensations assaulting him. He grunted and rose on his arms, taking her with a ruthless ardor that she greeted with avid delight.

But even while his primitive self commanded his actions, he never forgot what this incandescent joining meant.

Sally was his. She was his at last. And the knowledge lit his world with golden fire.

CHAPTER ELEVEN

*S*ally felt swept up into the whirlwind, hurled high into a brilliant sky. The years of dutiful and awkward congress with Norwood—and not particularly frequent congress at that—hadn't prepared her for this passionate storm. All she could do was cling to Charles and hope to heaven she survived the onslaught of hectic pleasure.

Charles thrust again, and she clenched around him. She loved the feeling of sublime closeness every time his body joined with hers. She curled her hands over his shoulders and tilted toward him. The change in position sparked a sizzling surge of heat.

"Come for me," he crooned in her ear, the words escaping in unsteady gasps.

"Come?" she asked, although after the unprecedented explosion of delight when he'd kissed her between the legs, she had an idea what that might mean. His actions had seemed outlandish, until the first wave crashed through her.

Now her body tightened toward something very like that spiraling release, but what built in her was even more powerful. Perhaps because this time, Charles was with her.

The ripples melted together into a tightening coil. Through her gathering crisis, she became aware that his movements became less controlled with every thrust. The fiery, inescapable intimacy of this connection was unlike anything she'd ever known.

"Yes, for God's sake," he rasped, and bent to kiss her with a clumsiness that made her heart cramp. She loved knowing that this union left him shaken and vulnerable, too. She lifted her hips to meet him, as lips, teeth and tongues clashed in a passionate battle.

Charles plunged deep, and Sally's world flared into searing white lightning.

She cried out over his guttural groan of satisfaction, and she dissolved into a cataclysm of dazzling pleasure. A gush of warmth inside her told her that he had found release. Her grip on his back tightened, as she tumbled through the fiery stars.

Through her shuddering reaction, she felt him jerk again. Then he withdrew and collapsed at her side, one powerful arm lashed around her to save her toppling to the floor.

"This chair isn't designed for two," she said, once she caught her breath, unsure whether her voice would work at all. Her throat was scratchy as if she'd screamed through every second of her headlong pleasure.

Who knew? Perhaps she had screamed. She'd been lost to everything but Charles's thundering possession.

An unsteady laugh escaped him.

Curious, she turned her head to survey him. By now, her eyes had adjusted to the lack of light. He looked happy—and at peace in a way she'd never seen before. He was so handsome that her exhausted heart skipped a beat. His eyes were heavy with satisfaction. His hair was rumpled and fell tangled over his forehead. His white shirt gaped open, giving her a glimpse of his hair-roughened chest.

What a magnificent lover this secret interlude had delivered to her.

She smoothed a rich brown lock back from his forehead. "What is it?"

Amusement lit his eyes to burnt toffee. "After what we just did, I hoped I might hear something a little more sentimental."

She frowned, even as a flood of foolish endearments and praise rose to her lips. Despite what they'd done together, she bit the words back.

Why? Shyness. Uncertainty. And the reluctant awareness that the events of their enchanted afternoon belonged only to this time and place. "But it's not made for two."

"No." Something in his eyes told her that he guessed how she struggled against saying too much. "If you turn around and fit yourself against me, we'll manage very well indeed. But first…"

He leaned forward and kissed her. A tender kiss with none of the tumultuous passion that had just transported her to paradise.

So why should this almost chaste kiss have the power to slice her heart in two?

She blinked away foolish tears and hoped the gloom hid them from Charles.

Small hope. He cupped her face and kissed her again with more of the poignant tenderness that vanquished all her defenses. "Lie with me, my darling, just for a few moments."

Sally struggled to remember that this was a mere interlude, and once they left this house, the rest of her life waited to claim her. The rest of her life held no place for this breathtaking lover, years younger than her.

She braced herself to speak the fatal name. "But if Meg…"

"She said she'd be a couple of hours."

"We need to talk." But the shameful truth was that Sally didn't want to talk. Not yet. Not ever, although she knew that was an impossible wish.

"Yes, we do." His expression turned somber, and she shivered as if a ghost passed through the air above her. "But not this very minute."

For a long interval, she stared into his face, tracing every inch with her eyes so that she could carve him on her heart just as he looked now. How could she deny him? He offered her an irresistible chance to linger in this golden heaven, even if just for a little while.

Trouble lay ahead, but trouble could wait.

She gave him a tentative smile, then squirmed around until her back pressed into his chest. His musky male scent surrounded her, as he drew her into the shelter of his body and shaped one possessive hand around her breast.

"I won't let you fall," he murmured in her ear, making her shiver as his breath brushed across her skin.

Silly girl she was, she so wanted to believe him. Which was absurd when she'd just fallen most convincingly.

But that unwelcome thought couldn't pierce her contentment as she cuddled up against Charles. She rested in the arms of the man she loved. For now, that was enough.

Charles stirred and opened his eyes to impenetrable

blackness. There was no interval of confusion or disorientation. His beloved, warm and soft and messy after their wild, astonishing, unforgettable encounter, slept with him.

He buried his nose in the soft tumble of her hair, breathing deeply of her intoxicating female scent. He felt drunk on Sally Cowan. Even in his most extravagant dreams, he'd never imagined that she'd give herself to him with such sweetness and generosity.

He had no idea what time it was, and nothing on God's green earth could lure him away from Sally to find his coat and dig his watch out of the pocket. He felt pleasantly weary, every muscle weighted with sleep and lingering satisfaction.

After that astounding climax, they both must have tumbled into a deep sleep. The chaise, which had earlier seemed cramped, now seemed just right. Sally's long slender body fit against his as if she'd been created to lie in his arms.

They were still dressed, at least in theory. Her skirts bunched against his thighs, and her bodice drooped to give him access to her pretty bosom. He'd managed to button his breeches before he dozed off, and his crumpled shirt lay loose around his hips.

With a stab of surprise, he realized he hadn't even delayed to take off his boots. He'd wanted her too much to think of anything else.

He tightened his grip on her waist, and his hand curled more firmly around her breast. He loved her neat little breasts with their tight, pink nipples. Nipples that tasted like strawberries.

A reminiscent smile curved his lips, as his mind turned to coaxing Sally into another bout. Idly his thumb toyed with the pointed peak, and he bumped his hips against her bottom. His cock rose hard and heavy, eager to be inside her once more.

He still couldn't quite believe what had happened. Amazing how a man's fate could turn upon a sixpence. He'd started the day wanting to cut his throat because he was convinced he'd lost her forever. Now he lay crammed up against his darling, basking in a happiness he'd never known before.

What a rare, extraordinary gift that happiness was. Although the real gift was the woman in his arms.

Sally shifted subtly so her tangled hair drifted across his shoulder. Her hand rose to cup his hand where it held her breast. His smile widened, as he tilted his head to kiss the lushly scented curve where her neck met her shoulder. She smelled of crushed flowers and female satisfaction—and a trace of sweat.

She made a drowsy sound of appreciation and shifted back against him. Then startling him, she suddenly went rigid and wriggled until she broke out of his hold.

With a cry, she tumbled off the narrow chaise and ended up crouching on the floor beside him.

"Oh, no. Oh, no. Oh, no. What have we done? Charles, what have we done?"

He couldn't see her face through the darkness, but her distraught voice chilled his skin with foreboding. He sat up and fumbled to touch her, but his hand met only air.

"Sally—"

"I can't believe this has happened. It's a complete disaster."

Damn it. "What the devil? Of course it's not a disaster," he snapped.

The shift from somnolent contentment was too abrupt. He struggled to see her through the shadows.

"But you're going to marry Meg," she said, her voice cracking.

His rare temper flared, although he supposed he should have expected something like this. He surged to his feet and crossed to the window. His shaking hands took too long to find the catch for the shutters. When at last he did, he flung them wide, letting bright moonlight flood the room.

"Credit me with some scrap of honor, Sally," he said coldly, turning back to face her. "As though I'd touch you if I harbored any intentions toward your niece."

Sally stumbled to her feet. Despite his current impulse to give her a good shake until she saw sense, his heart crashed against his ribs at the delectable picture she presented. She might have tugged her bodice up to restore her modesty, but she still looked deliciously rumpled. Her thick mane of dark gold hair cascaded over her shoulders, and the moonlight was bright enough to reveal her full, kiss-swollen lips. "You've courted her for weeks."

He ground his teeth and prowled across to the side-board where he used the tinderbox to light a candle. "No, by God, I haven't."

He was almost sorry when the flame flickered into life and illuminated Sally's expression in its full glory. She looked furious.

Worse, she looked ashamed.

Regret and frustration slammed into him, stole the breath from his lungs. What the hell was going on? He'd clearly been a complete blockhead to imagine that during these incandescent hours, they'd established an understanding.

"Don't lie." She folded her arms and surveyed him with angry disbelief.

"I don't lie." Ice edged his voice.

She dismissed his statement with a sweeping gesture. "You made a point of singling her out. For pity's sake, you were at every event we attended. What else is that but the behavior of a suitor?"

He growled deep in his throat. "Of course I was a suitor. I was courting you."

If he'd hoped his declaration might mollify her, he was to be disappointed. She made a disgusted sound and backed away. After their closeness, her reaction was doubly cruel. When he'd been inside her, he felt like they shared a heartbeat.

She shook her head. "I don't believe it."

"Why not? It's true." His eyes narrowed as he went on the attack. "And if you're so bloody convinced that I mean to marry your niece, what in hell do you mean by having your wicked way with me this afternoon?"

Even in the candlelight, he saw the hectic flush that flooded her face. "You…you seduced me."

He arched his eyebrows and watched her steadily, until her eyes flickered down and she turned her face away. "I'm sorry," she mumbled. "That wasn't fair."

"No, it wasn't."

She wrung her hands like a wronged woman in a play. "I can't explain what came over me. I must have been mad."

"No more than I." He shook his head and stepped forward to quiet those nervous hands. His anger receded a little. He hated to see her so tormented. "I wanted you. You wanted me. It's purely natural that we succumbed to our passion."

For one charged second, she accepted his touch, and he wondered if everything would be all right. Then she wrenched away. "It might be natural, but it's wrong."

"Why the hell is it wrong?"

"Well, let's start with Meg." Unshed tears shone in Sally's eyes as she stared up at him.

He couldn't help contrasting this stricken creature with the glowing woman who had found her pleasure with him deep inside her. Regret tasted sour in his mouth. He wanted that glowing woman back.

"What about Meg?"

"She's set her heart on marrying you."

Charles gave a dismissive snort. "Miss Meg is no more interested in marrying me than I am in marrying her. I'd bore her stiff within a week—if I managed to winkle her out of my stables for a conversation, that is."

Sally's jaw set with familiar stubbornness. "You can't know that she doesn't want to marry you."

"Yes, I can." He bared his teeth in a humorless smile. "She told me."

Astonishment widened Sally's eyes. "When?"

"The night you sent us off to the long gallery with matchmaking in mind." Something that had rankled for days found voice. "Why in Hades did you shove me at your niece when you wanted me for yourself?"

He saw her consider denying his statement, but something in his face must have deterred her from another lie. "You two would be perfect together."

"We'd be a bloody catastrophe." He sighed and ran his hand through his hair. "Meg knows it. I know it. If you turned your sharp mind to reality instead of whatever damned lunacy is possessing you, you'd know it, too."

"Meg likes you."

"I like her, too. But I don't want to marry her." His voice turned urgent. He was watching his every hope crumbling to dust in front of him. "I want to marry you. Meg wants me to marry you."

Anger flared in Sally's eyes, although he knew her

well enough to see that fear fueled much of her temper. "How kind of you both to dispose of my future."

He ignored the sarcasm and dared a step closer. "I most ardently hope you'll entrust that future to me, Sally."

"I know you want to marry Meg," she said steadily. "I heard you talking to Silas about your proposal."

He made a frustrated sound. "I was talking about my proposal to you, my sweet henwit. For the tenth time, I don't want to marry your niece. I want to marry *you*. Will you marry me, Sally?"

"No." She stepped away, shaking her head in frantic denial, and this time she couldn't hide the fright glittering in her eyes. "It's impossible."

"Why?" God give him patience. He sucked in a deep breath. "After what just happened, you can't deny that we're made for each other."

He'd known that from the first. Why couldn't she see that, too?

"My behavior is inexcusable, but what we did hasn't changed my mind about not marrying again, Sir Charles." She drew herself up to her full height and responded in a frigid voice. "Your proposal is unwelcome."

Sir Charles again, was it? He narrowed his eyes, even as his gut cramped in instinctive denial. She couldn't mean it. He refused to believe her.

This wasn't the truth. He'd known the truth when

she quivered around him in ecstasy, and wrapped him in her arms as if she'd never let him go.

Damn her, she wasn't going to get away so easily. His tone turned silky. "And what if you bear my child as a result of today's recklessness?"

CHAPTER TWELVE

*C*ould this awful day get any worse? The misery was more excruciating because for that foolish, transfiguring, unforgettable time in his arms, Sally had been happier than she'd ever been in her life.

She bit back a moan when Charles mentioned a baby, even as her hand settled where her crumpled green dress covered her useless womb. He couldn't know how his questions stabbed at her. He wasn't a spiteful man, no matter how angry he might be.

With justice.

Her behavior must strike him as capricious to the point of lunacy. She'd tumbled into his arms with no resistance at all, and now, when the harm was well and truly done, she rejected his attempts to restore her honor.

How she regretted succumbing to him. But when

he'd kissed her, surprise had caught her defenseless, and all common sense had fled. She'd just wanted and longed. And feared that this might be her only chance to know the touch of the man she loved.

She'd given no consideration to consequences. God forgive her, she hadn't even spared a thought for Meg.

Although at least it now seemed that Meg didn't want to marry Sir Charles.

Small consolation when Sally stood before him and denied what she wanted more than anything else in the world.

"You don't need to sacrifice yourself to save my good name," she said sourly. "I'm barren. In nearly ten years of marriage, there was no sign of a child."

He frowned, tucking in his shirt with jerky movements. "Haven't you heard a word I've said? I want to marry you. I wanted you from the moment I first saw you."

Oh, if only there was somewhere to run. She loathed seeing how she hurt him. Witnessing his confusion was almost worse than suffering her own. And right now, she felt like her heart broke into a thousand jagged pieces. "I'm sorry. I can't accept."

She waited for an explosion of masculine pique. Norwood had loathed her challenging him.

But then Norwood had been a bully, and Charles Kinglake wasn't.

He spread his hands. "Why?"

She gave a heavy sigh. Surely he could see she was

an utterly unsuitable wife for him. It was blatantly and excruciatingly obvious to her. "So many reasons."

"Name them. You can't still think Meg and I have some sort of understanding. For God's sake, she left us alone here so we could sort out our differences."

"For which she's earned a trip home to her parents, after I've given her a good scolding," Sally said bitterly, resenting her niece's interference in matters that were none of her concern.

"She meant well."

"And meaning well, she's caused a complete mess."

He flinched, and she raised a hand to soothe the sting of her unguarded words, until she recalled touching him wasn't a good idea.

His wide shoulders rose and fell as he sucked in a deep breath. She could tell he fought to keep his deep voice steady. "Explain to me why you can't accept my proposal. After what just happened, you'll never convince me that you don't want me."

She'd dearly love to disown her desire, but given how swiftly she'd yielded, she'd look even more ridiculous if she claimed indifference. Although the damage was already done, she hitched her bodice higher in an attempt to bolster her dignity. "I'm too old for you."

"Tosh. It's a couple of years."

"Enough to count."

"Not with me. Is that the best you can do?"

"And I can't bear you children."

The skeptical arch of his dark eyebrows made her

want to hit him. "Have you slept with anyone other than your husband?"

She raised her chin. "Yes."

He looked stricken. "Who?"

Her lips tightened with impatience. "You, of course."

His grunt of laughter was unamused. "Of course. Anyone else?"

"Sir Charles—" she began, hard-won composure starting to fray.

"You may as well tell me." He sighed and ran his hand through his hair, leaving it even more ruffled. And making him look even more irresistible, curse him. "I know anyway."

"And just what do you think you know, sir?"

"You were almost innocent in my arms." His lips curled in a wry smile. "You certainly didn't act like a woman practiced in the sensual arts."

Despite everything, his criticism of her performance as a lover made her cringe. "Well, I'm sorry if my inexperience was a problem."

"There was no problem, my darling." He reached out briefly to touch her cheek. She told herself to step away, but the gesture's tenderness kept her unmoving under his hand. "What we did was a revelation. At least for me. I hope it was for you, too."

Sally bit her lip, wanting to argue, but unable to speak the lie that surely would send him away forever. Although it was kinder to both of them if she sundered this bond now, rather than letting the misery go on and on.

He was close enough for her to catch his scent, a sensual reminder of all the wonderful things he'd done to her, and would never do again. She blinked back searing tears.

The slight smile lingering, he subjected her to a searching look. "I wouldn't be quite so sure you're incapable of bearing children. The difficulty may have been Norwood's."

"But what if I am barren?" she persisted, beating down the fragile seedling of hope Charles's words coaxed into the light. It had taken her years to accept she'd never have a baby. She couldn't survive coming to terms with that disappointment a second time.

Charles shrugged and took her hand. She was so confused and unhappy, she didn't pull free. She must be strong and send him away, she knew. But his touch made her feel so warm and alive, while life without him promised nothing but eternal arctic cold.

"The title doesn't end with me. With four married sisters, I have more nephews than I can keep track of. If I have no son to inherit, I can live with that. Perhaps we can adopt needy orphans, or assist with all those nieces and nephews. Or we can just find contentment in each other. Travel. Collect art. Breed dogs." The smile widened. "I don't really care, as long as you're with me."

"You make it sound so tempting." Her starving heart

longed toward what he said like a man dying of thirst longed for a clear stream. But the sheer power of that longing was enough to show her that she couldn't accept.

Sally wasn't just saying no to Charles for his sake, but for her own. She'd been trapped in an unequal marriage. She knew the harrowing price such a marriage demanded.

He frowned. He was smart enough to guess that her reply wasn't the prelude to acceptance. "Then say yes."

"I spent nearly ten years with a man who did his best to make me feel inadequate." When she withdrew her hand, she was surprised it didn't tremble. "I swore I'd never do that again."

Anger flashed in Charles's eyes, made them blaze russet. "I'll never do that to you."

She shook her head. "No, I know you wouldn't. At least not on purpose. But eventually you'll regret marrying your older, barren wife. And in trying to hide your disappointment with your choice, you'd hurt me more than you would if you showed it openly."

"That's the stupidest bloody thing I've ever heard." One large hand made a frustrated gesture. "I wouldn't be hiding any damned disappointment, because I wouldn't be feeling it."

"So you say now."

He sighed again. She knew he didn't understand— but then she was older and wiser, which was the problem.

His voice turned low and persuasive. "Sally, I'm not a fickle man. I've never before met a woman I want to marry. Now I've found you, I won't give you up lightly."

She shook her head and backed away until she bumped the table behind her. She started and stumbled, and Charles moved quickly to catch her elbow. "My love, you're tired and upset. Let's leave this for now."

His touch and the gentleness in his voice, worse, the way he called her his love, shuddered through her like a blow. "No," she said in a choked voice. "You've proposed, and I've declined. There's nothing to gain from pursuing this."

His grip tightened. "I won't accept that."

She raised her head and studied his chiseled features. He looked so lost and baffled. "You must."

His expression turned stern. "So if that's true and you want nothing more to do with me, why did you give yourself to me?"

The stark question lay between them like a challenge. After what they'd shared, she owed him honesty.

She swallowed. Her throat felt like it was lined with broken glass. It hurt to speak, and her voice emerged low and unsteady. "I think because for a couple of hours, I wanted the dream to come true. It was disgraceful of me, but I've been so lonely, and you offered me the chance to discover a pleasure I'd never known."

Even in the candlelight, she saw him go white. He let her go abruptly, as if she'd burned him.

"So this was nothing more to you than an experiment?" The anger in his voice lacerated her.

He was wrong, so wrong. But if she told him that she'd never felt so close to anyone in her life, and that the thought of never experiencing that closeness again made her want to die, he'd ask her to marry him again. And whatever her aching heart might want, her mind knew that way lay disaster.

Ten years of Norwood's neglect and contempt had crushed her spirit nearly into the ground. She'd survived. She wouldn't survive knowing she let Charles down. How could she bear to see him realize that marrying her was a mistake?

She hadn't loved her husband. She loved Charles. Love made everything worse.

So she stiffened her spine and looked him in the eyes, as difficult as that was. And her voice emerged with only a small wobble. "A very nice experiment."

"Nice..." He spat the word like a curse. "Sally, I love you. Doesn't that mean anything to you?"

He loved her?

She fought against believing him, even as she had to beat back the vow that rose in response to his. "Love..." she whispered.

"Yes, *love,* Sally."

She wished he didn't sound so sure. Every time she thought she'd reached the limits of her endurance, there was something worse to come. She reminded herself again that she wasn't the right wife for Charles Kinglake.

"Charles…" she said helplessly. Then on a burst of exasperation, "Where the devil is Meg? Surely she can't mean to leave us here all night."

When she didn't respond to his declaration with a declaration of her own, Charles's expression turned frozen. But God help her, she was familiar enough with strategies for concealing pain to know how he suffered. She reminded herself that he'd suffer worse and longer, if he saddled himself with the wrong wife.

"She said a couple of hours." He bit out each word. "But it must be getting near midnight."

"What time is it?"

With an uncharacteristically jerky step, he crossed to pick up his coat and fish out his pocket watch. "A quarter to eight."

She'd imagined it was later. She felt like she'd lived through an entire lifetime since Meg had stolen away in Charles's curricle.

"I hope she's all right." It was almost a relief to think about Meg, instead of two broken hearts and the desolate future. "What did she say to you about what she planned?"

"Nothing. This prank took me as much by surprise as it did you." He sent her a grim glance. "And I don't care whether you believe that. It's the truth."

She'd always been conscious of the difference in

their ages. But right now, he looked old and tired in a way she'd never seen before. Guilt stabbed her that her sinful weakness for him had brought about this misery.

"Of course I believe you," she said in a small voice, hating how she hurt him. "I'm sorry, Charles. I'm sorry for everything."

"So am I."

His flat tone opened a new rift in her heart. She was under no illusions how the loss of his friendship would devastate her. From the beginning, his companionship had enriched her life. Now she'd lost his regard, and she wanted to sit down and cry like an abandoned child.

"This will probably be our last chance for a private discussion." Charles still spoke with scrupulous courtesy, so that every word hit her like a bullet. "If there are…consequences from this afternoon, will you tell me?"

"Yes," she said almost soundlessly. "But I'm sure you're safe."

Anger tightened his features, deepened the lines between his nose and mouth, but his response emerged with more frigid politeness. "I won't have any child of mine born without knowing its father."

She bit her lip so hard, she drew blood and told herself that it was better this way. One clean cut, and all temptation was excised from her life.

But it didn't feel better. It felt like someone hacked off her leg with a blunt knife, leaving her crippled forever. "You're an honorable man, Charles. I never thought you were anything else."

His mouth was a long thin line, and that muscle danced in his cheek again, proof of strong emotion. "I don't feel honorable right now."

She looked away and blinked back another surge of acrid tears. "I know," she whispered. "But you've done nothing wrong."

Whereas she, through her selfishness, had made him hellishly unhappy. She prayed the wound wasn't mortal. She wished she could doubt the depth of his misery, but it was impossible. When he said he loved her, he meant it.

She curled her fingers into her palms until the nails scored her skin. "I…I'd really like to be alone for a little while."

"There are beds upstairs." He still sounded like a stranger.

"No, I'd rather wait down here," she muttered, as the memory of how he'd swept her up in his arms flashed through her mind. He'd been so hungry for her, he hadn't taken the time to find a bedroom. For heaven's sake, they'd both been so lost to passion, they hadn't even undressed.

No, she couldn't dwell on those heated, transforming moments. That way lay madness.

"I'll go into the next room," he said.

"No…" She reached out to stop him, before she remembered she'd lost the right to touch him.

The gaze he leveled upon her was distant. "I'd prefer that, if you don't mind."

She braced against his coldness. He sounded worse than a stranger. He sounded like he hated her.

"I'll see if I can find us something to eat. I know there's some brandy in the cellars."

The thought of food made her gag. "No, thank you."

"Would you like a fire?"

"No, no, it's a warm night." His attempts to ensure her wellbeing made her want to scream.

"If Meg isn't back by dawn, I'll set out for Upton." He still spoke in that distant voice. "It's ten miles away, but I should find help there."

Sally made herself stand up straight. "I want to box the chit's ears," she said bitterly. Although she couldn't blame her niece for this almighty mess. It was all her fault.

"No doubt." Charles gave her a chilly bow. "Then I'll wish you good night."

"Thank you."

She watched him go through to the hall, then return with her pelisse which he dropped over the back of a chair. "In case it gets cold later."

"Thank you," she said again, and crossed the room to look out the window at the moon. After a moment's bristling silence, she heard him leave again.

She didn't look around. She couldn't bear for him to see her tears.

CHAPTER THIRTEEN

*C*harles stirred from his uneasy doze to hear the outside door opening behind him. He shifted and groaned. He was too tall to sleep in a chair —and a hard chair at that.

"Sir Charles?" Meg stood on the threshold, carrying one of the lanterns from his curricle. She looked windswept and tired, but unharmed, thank God.

"Miss Meg," he said, standing up, buttoning his coat.

"Where's Aunt Sally?"

"Asleep in the next room." He checked his watch. It was nearly eleven o'clock. "Where the devil have you been?"

"I got… Oh, there you are, Aunt Sally."

"Are you all right, Meg?" she asked, coming through from the room where she and Charles had made love.

After all that had happened between them, seeing

Sally felt like a punch to the solar plexus. On a wave of bitter misery, the events of the night rushed toward him. The wonder of having her in his arms, the sweetness of her surrender, followed by those devastating words that pulverized his every hope.

His hungry eyes ate up the sight of her. She'd put on her pelisse and found enough pins to tidy her hair. She looked almost respectable. But her lovely face was pallid and drawn, and the thickness in her voice revealed that she'd been crying.

Hell, he hated that he'd made her cry. His hands clenched into useless fists at his sides as if he prepared to fight some unnamed foe. Although the tragic truth was that when it came to his battle to win this exquisite woman, the dragons had emerged victorious.

"Yes, I'm fine," the girl said, coming fully inside and shutting the heavy door behind her.

"Then you have no excuse for not coming back to get us," Sally said coldly. "Leaving us here was wicked and irresponsible, but to stay away long enough to threaten to bring a scandal down on our heads is unforgivable."

The rebuke clearly startled Meg. "I only intended to be a little while."

"Even that was reprehensible enough. So why were you so long?"

"I…I got lost." Meg, who became less chirpy with every second, placed the lantern on a side table. The hand carrying it had shown an increasing tendency to shake.

Charles couldn't find the heart to be angry with her. "Meg, I warned you that the estate was isolated and hard to find."

She cast him an apologetic glance. "I know you did. I meant to call on Perdita, then come back. But the lanes around here are a maze. I couldn't find Perdita's house, and it's only good luck that I found my way back here at all."

"We should be thankful for small mercies, then," Sally said. "I've been worried sick that you'd been attacked or injured."

"I'm sorry, Aunt," Meg said in a subdued voice. She cast a glance at Charles, but he shook his head, wishing to heaven that her tricks had resulted in a different outcome. "I'd hoped if you had a chance to be alone, you'd reach an understanding."

He waited for Sally to flare up, but her voice remained calm. Unnaturally calm, he couldn't help thinking. "The only understanding we've come to is that I have a rattle-pate niece, unfit for polite society."

"I thought…"

Sally didn't let her finish. "You'll have plenty of time for thinking back under your father's roof, my girl."

Meg looked aghast. "You can't send me home."

"I can and I will." When she folded her arms, Sally looked as implacable as a stone statue. "Just be grateful that for my sake as well as yours, I won't tell your father the disgraceful truth."

"It's not fair to send me away." Meg suddenly sounded so young, Charles almost felt sorry for her.

"Miss Meg, I know you meant well today, but perhaps this is for the best," he said gently.

"You've proven yourself unworthy of my trust. You've acted in a way that imperiled yourself, not to mention endangered my reputation and Sir Charles's good name. I just pray we all get out of this without becoming the talk of the Town."

Sally still spoke in that even, unemotional voice that somehow was worse than if she lost her temper. She'd spoken in just such a tone when she'd dashed all his hopes for happiness. Meg seemed to shrink under every measured, critical word.

"There's absolutely no need for anybody else to know about this," he reminded Sally.

"I hope not." Sally didn't look at him. "Now tell me you haven't damaged Sir Charles's rig or horses."

The implied insult to her driving skills made Meg fire up. "Of course I didn't. I'd never injure a horse."

"It's a pity you don't devote some of your care for horses to people, Meg." Sally sounded deathly tired and sad and defeated.

He'd sell his soul for the right to comfort her, but he was the last person she'd turn to. His gut cramped with stabbing regret. He loathed the desolation he heard in her voice. A desolation he knew that he, not Meg, had caused, however disappointed she was in her niece.

"Apologize to Sir Charles, then for pity's sake, let us leave this place. With any luck, they'll still have our rooms at the Angel."

The picture of remorse, Meg turned to Charles. "I'm dreadfully sorry, Sir Charles. I hope you can forgive me."

How could he bear a grudge? In her harebrained fashion, she'd tried to help him. It wasn't her fault everything had come to ruin and despair. He nodded and summoned up a smile. "Of course I forgive you, Miss Meg."

"You're too good," Meg said in a choked voice.

"At least you're not hurt," Charles said. "We were worried about you."

"He is too good," Sally said, casting him a narrow-eyed glance before she faced Meg again. "I hope you know how you've let me down, and you'll learn from this debacle never to interfere again in matters you're too young to understand."

With a pleading expression, Meg stepped toward her aunt. "I am so very, very sorry, Aunt Sally." The tears she'd been bravely fighting started to pour down her cheeks. "If I've hurt you in any way, I'll…I'll go into a convent and never speak to anyone ever again."

The extravagant claim at last pierced Sally's severe manner. To Charles's relief, her lips quirked in a frail imitation of her usual brilliant smile. She'd been holding herself so stiffly that he'd feared she must break. At least now she looked human and not like a marble deity.

"There's no need to go overboard. If we ban you from the stables for a year, that should be punishment enough."

"Ban me from…" Meg's face brightened with relief. "You're having a joke."

"I am." She opened her arms to her niece. "Now come and give me a hug, you dreadful child."

Meg stumbled forward to sob a litany of promises and apologies into her aunt's shoulder. When she pulled away, she was sniffing and breathing unsteadily. "I'm so, so sorry."

Sally's smile was so disconsolate, Charles wanted to smash something. She dug in her pocket for a handkerchief which she passed to her niece. "We'll say no more about it."

Meg choked out, "What about the scandal?"

"We'll deal with that if we must," Charles said firmly. At the moment, gossip was the least of his worries. "At those big coaching inns, travelers come and go at all hours. If we three turn up past midnight, I doubt questions will be asked."

Meg wiped her face and looked a little more cheerful. She shot her aunt a glance under her lashes. "So if there's no scandal, can I stay with you in London?"

"I'm sorry, Meg." Sally shook her head. Charles hated to see her return to looking like the figure of justice carved on a courthouse. "You've shown I can't trust you. You're safer with your father and mother."

Meg's face fell. "Aunt…"

Charles bit back the impulse to interfere. He had no right to ask Sally to relent. He had no rights where Sally was concerned at all, blast it all to hell.

"My mind is made up." Sally turned away to find her bonnet. She tied it on, then opened the door, letting the moonlight flood in. "Shall we go?"

Feeling like he bore the weight of the world on his shoulders, Charles collected his hat. He'd experienced such extremes of emotion since he'd come into this house. Right now, he hoped to God he never saw the lovely little hunting box again. He had a bloody good mind to demolish it, so it lay in ruins along with his every hope of happiness.

With the grim awareness that once they left *Sans Souci*, Sally was lost to him forever, he lifted the lantern. As Sally headed outside, he offered his arm to Meg.

"Sir Charles, I wanted…" Meg muttered under her breath, as she hooked her hand around his bent elbow.

"So did I, Meg," he said in a bleak voice. "But I made a complete mess of everything."

She looked up at him hopefully. "But surely you can fix it?"

He watched Sally trudge across the gravel to the carriage. She usually rushed at life with a verve he found irresistible. But tonight he couldn't mistake the slump of her shoulders and the way every step seemed an effort.

"No," he said in a flat voice that concealed the rage and devastation in his heart. "No, some things are broken forever."

CHAPTER FOURTEEN

*S*ally sighed and put aside her embroidery. She'd never been much good at needlework, and she'd only picked it up this afternoon because every other distraction had failed to…distract her. She lifted the cup of tea her butler had poured half an hour ago.

"Ugh." It was ice cold. She blinked back tears. Over the last week, everything made her cry, even something as trivial as a cold cup of tea.

"For pity's sake, you look as down in the dumps as Meg does." Wearing a disapproving expression, Morwenna appeared in the drawing room's doorway. "This house has turned into a dratted mausoleum lately."

"I'm sorry. I'm a little blue-deviled," Sally said, mustering a smile for her friend. "You, on the other hand, look marvelous. Is that a new dress?"

She struggled to sound the way she used to, as if she hadn't a care in the world. Even in her own ears, the attempt was an abject failure.

Still, it was cheering to see Morwenna in such fine fettle. Tonight her friend wore a rich azure taffeta gown that matched her lovely eyes, and her silky, ruler-straight black hair was dressed with pearls and roses and ribbons. Sally recalled the grieving wraith from last November who had reluctantly agreed to join in the London adventure.

"Yes, it is. Lord Garson is taking me to the opera."

"Lucky you." Sally glanced out and noticed that twilight had crept in. She must have been sitting in here brooding alone for hours.

Another gray day had passed, with her barely aware of anything beyond her own wretchedness. Every day lately was gray, whatever the weather was like.

The worst of her unhappiness over losing Charles would fade with time. That was how life worked, wasn't it? Nothing lasted forever. They could now get on with forgetting each other.

In the meantime, she just had to endure. She'd endured a disagreeable marriage. Surely her love for someone she'd known a mere matter of weeks would eventually change from present anguish to wistful memory.

Morwenna came into the room and sank into a brocade chair opposite the sofa where Sally sat. "You're welcome to join us if you like."

"I'm not dressed to go out." She indicated the sprigged muslin she'd put on this morning.

"Garson won't be here for another half hour. You have plenty of time to change."

"No, thank you. I feel like a quiet night." At the opera, she'd have to pretend she was still witty, sparkly, insouciant Sally Cowan. Worse, at the opera, she was likely to see Sir Charles Kinglake. She'd rather take her embroidery needle and poke out her eye than risk that.

Impatience lit Morwenna's eyes to sapphire. "You've felt like a quiet night ever since you got back from Shelton Abbey a week ago."

Sally shrugged. "Now I'm not chaperoning Meg to any parties, there's no great necessity for me to dance the night away."

"Do you really mean to send her home tomorrow?"

"She's lucky I didn't send her home the day we returned to London."

Sally had relented enough to let Meg stay to say goodbye to her friends. Sally had even allowed her to attend the theatre, a musicale, and a ball—although not the one given by the new Duchess of Sedgemoor. She didn't want people commenting on the girl's sudden withdrawal from society, and perhaps seeking some scandalous reason to explain it.

Like a coward, instead of accompanying her niece, she'd made sure Fenella or Helena kept her on a short rein. But given Meg's continuing flood of apologies, she was almost sure the girl had learned her lesson and wouldn't do anything outrageous.

"Are you ever going to tell me what happened at the house party?" Morwenna's expression was concerned. "I've left you alone so far, because it was clear you were in a state when you arrived back. But you've been in a funk for a week now, and it might help you to talk about what's upset you. I've asked Caro and Helena, but they claim ignorance."

Sally rose on a surge of temper. "You have no business prying."

"I do when you're so unhappy, and Meg's going back to Hampshire." Morwenna remained calm under Sally's glare. "And Sir Charles Kinglake, who has been a constant presence in our lives since he came to London, hasn't been seen in public for a week, and now the word is that he's closing up his house and going to Italy."

"Italy," Sally said on the ghost of a sound, forgetting all about her squabble with Morwenna.

"That's what people are saying."

"Oh," Sally said shakily, turning away toward the window so Morwenna wouldn't see her silly tears.

It was the height of capriciousness to regret that Charles was leaving England. She'd said no to his proposal. She'd sent him away. He'd been gentleman enough to heed her. And so far no whisper of scandal had emerged about their dalliance. Apart from the jagged wound in her heart, the matter was concluded.

But something about the thought of him so very far away made her want to cry her eyes out.

"Sally?" She felt Morwenna's cool touch on her arm. "Did Sir Charles and Meg do something terrible in Leicestershire?"

"No." Although they had. Meg had played a stupid, childish trick, and Charles had lured Sally into finding a pleasure she'd never known. Worse, he'd said he loved her.

Right now, that seemed the cruelest cut of all.

Morwenna's tone remained gentle but uncompromising. "Then why are you sending Meg back to her father, and why have you turned into a hermit, and why is Sir Charles moving to the Continent?"

Sally fumbled for her handkerchief and avoided Morwenna's gaze. "There's nothing to tell."

"Obviously there's lots to tell, or you wouldn't be crying. Don't you trust me?"

Why the devil were people always asking her that? The only person she really didn't trust was herself. "Of course I do."

"Then?"

On a shuddering sob, Sally gave up the struggle. "It's so hard to explain."

"Try."

She straightened and drew an unsteady breath. "Everything is a complete mess."

"Let me guess." Morwenna led her back to the sofa and sat beside her, holding her hand. "Meg and Sir

Charles were caught in a compromising position, and he refuses to do the right thing and restore her reputation."

Sally's brief laugh was devoid of amusement. "No, it's much worse than that."

"Worse?"

"Yes. It turns out I had everything wrong, from the very beginning. He doesn't want to marry Meg, and she doesn't want to marry him."

Morwenna sighed with relief. "I'm glad. To me, they never seemed right together. In fact, you and Sir Charles always seemed a better fit."

For one horrified moment, Sally stared at her friend. Then she released a choked breath and burst into the tears that had hovered all day.

How humiliating. Where was the proud woman who had kept up appearances all through her awful marriage? Love had turned her into a complete wreck. She buried her wet face in her shaking hands and struggled to control this outburst, but it was impossible.

"Oh, Sally, I hate to see you so miserable," Morwenna said, passing her a handkerchief.

Her friend's sympathy finally shattered Sally's reticence. In confused, broken sentences, she confessed the events of that trip back from Leicestershire, with the exception of her fall from grace on the chaise longue.

Sally wiped her stinging eyes and dragged in a broken breath. When she bit her lip, she tasted the salt of her tears. "So you can see why I have to send Meg away."

Morwenna's gaze was searching. Something in her expression hinted that she'd guessed more than conversation had taken place in the isolated hunting lodge. "She's behaved disgracefully, I agree. But on the other hand, you'd never have given Sir Charles the chance to declare himself if Meg hadn't taken a hand."

Sally stiffened and tried to summon her anger, but crying had left her weary to the point of exhaustion. Crying, and barely a wink of sleep over the last week. Whenever she drifted off, her mind returned to those rapturous, heartbreaking moments when Charles had moved inside her. She'd rather spend the night staring up at the ceiling and calling herself every name under the sun for her stupidity than revisit that passionate interlude.

"I didn't want him to declare himself," she muttered. She tore savagely at the lace handkerchief between her hands.

"Why not?" Morwenna cast her an unimpressed glance. "You're head over heels in love with him. Aren't you glad that he loves you, too?"

"I'm not…" She hadn't confessed her feelings for Charles either, but Morwenna knew her too well. Her shoulders slumped. "Oh, all right, yes. I do love him. But it's completely out of the question."

Morwenna shook her head in disbelief. "Sally, I think you're a lunatic."

Sally stood up and began to pace. "Didn't you listen to me? I'm older than he is."

"Only a few years. Not enough to matter. You've convinced yourself you're past the age of romance—I think because you can't bear the thought of being hurt again, after the hell Norwood put you through."

Sally stiffened. She hated to hear people refer to her failure as a wife. "His lordship was all that was correct."

Morwenna made a dismissive noise. "I didn't know Lord Norwood. But everything I've heard tells me he was a narrow-minded bully, too beef-witted to appreciate the wonderful wife fate placed in his care."

"I don't want to marry again," Sally said, too upset to call up any stronger defense of her late husband. Anyway, Morwenna was right.

"I can understand you feel like that. But you need to start looking at the facts. Sir Charles isn't anything like Norwood. For a start, Charles loves you."

"Stop saying that."

Morwenna stood up and faced her. "Why? It's true."

"He can't marry me." Sally stopped her restless marching about and scowled at her friend. "I'm barren."

Morwenna shrugged. "You said when you told him that, he wanted you anyway."

"I clearly said far too much."

Disgust weighted Morwenna's sigh. "Well, I'll tell you something, Sally Cowan. Right now I'm ashamed to own you as my friend."

Sally stepped back, startled at this sudden severity. "What?"

Morwenna made a sweeping gesture with one hand. "You're acting like a craven coward—when something I always admired about you is your indomitable spirit. You want that man, and he wants you. Yet you're too lily-livered to reach out your hand and seize your happiness. Instead you're wallowing in endless excuses. You'll end up drowning in them before you're done. And meanwhile, poor Meg goes home under a cloud, and Sir Charles packs up his broken heart and trudges around Florence and Venice, trying like the devil to forget you."

Sally's hands clenched at her sides. "What right have you to criticize me?"

Morwenna's face went pale, and the gloss of happiness melted away. Sally realized with a sick feeling that was all her friend's gaiety had ever been—a gloss hiding a wound that would never heal.

"Because real love is a gift beyond price and it's worth every risk. Because you've got a chance at finding happiness, and you're turning your back on it, without recognizing how inordinately lucky you are." Morwenna's voice trembled with overpowering emotion. "Because I had real love and I lost it, not because of anything I did, but just because that's the way the world turns. Honestly, Sally, I could give you a good slap."

Sally, jolted out of her self-centered dejection, stared aghast at Morwenna. "I'm so sorry. I hoped…"

"That I'd recovered from Robert's loss?" Morwenna's lips twisted into a bitter smile. "I know that would make life more comfortable for everyone. Probably for me, too. But you don't forget a man like Robert Nash, and real love doesn't easily let you go. If at all. Think about that, Sally, as you turn your back on Sir Charles."

Sally curled her hand over Morwenna's. Her friend was shaking with the force of her feelings. "But you and Lord Garson—"

"Get along well." She mustered a smile. Not a very convincing one. "He's a kind and good man, and I like him."

"I'd hoped you might find happiness again. These last weeks…"

Morwenna drew away and squared her shoulders. To her mortification, Sally acknowledged that the only truly courageous person in this room was Morwenna Nash.

"If Lord Garson asks me to marry him, I'll say yes. Kerenza needs a father, and I'm lonely and seeking a purpose beyond bringing up my daughter alone. I'd like more children. I'd like companionship and a man in my life. Nobody will ever replace Robert. But he's been gone more than four years, and I'm still young. I need to keep living. For Kerenza's sake, if nothing else."

Tears rose to Sally's eyes, and she pressed Morwenna's hand. "Your bravery puts me to shame."

Morwenna's eyes sharpened. "I hope so. Because having had love ripped away from me, I can't abide seeing you blithely tossing your chance to the side."

"I'm not…I'm not doing anything blithely."

Morwenna's expression softened with compassion. "I know, Sally."

The butler appeared at the door. "Lord Garson has called for Mrs Nash, my lady."

Morwenna's lips tightened, and she spoke in a low tone so the butler wouldn't hear. "Stop letting past miseries rule you, Sally. You're scared, I know, but fear makes for a cold bedfellow."

She tugged on her long satin gloves and mustered a smile when Garson came in and bowed to both of them. But as Sally watched her friend flirting with her openly bedazzled admirer, she couldn't help but play Morwenna's words over and over in her head.

Real love was worth every risk.

CHAPTER FIFTEEN

"*A* lady to see you, Sir Charles," his butler said from the library doorway.

Charles glanced up, an exquisite octavo edition of Petrarch's sonnets in his hand. He was sorting through the books he was sending on to Venice where he planned to rent a palazzo.

It was late, past midnight, but he wasn't sleeping much these days. The week had been hell. Giving up on his heart's desire made a man poor company.

"What lady?" he asked impatiently.

"She wouldn't say, sir. And heavy veils prevented me from assaying her identity." The butler cleared his throat. "She appears very eager to speak with you."

Brief curiosity surfaced, then sank back into the mire that his life had become lately. He put the Petrarch in a box and picked up another book.

"I don't have time for ladies right now," he said in a

flat tone. "Tell the wench, whoever she is, to go away. I'm surprised you didn't tell her yourself, Willis. You know I'm leaving in the morning."

"She asked me to give you this note."

With an irritated sigh, Charles put down the leather-bound book and lifted the scrap of paper from the salver Willis extended toward him.

Swiftly he unfolded the paper. He didn't know the writing, but what he saw made his heart swell with an emotion he hadn't felt since he'd left Leicestershire.

Sir, I have no right to your consideration, but I'd appreciate a moment of your time. S.

A cryptic message. Good news or bad?

Hope rushed through him and set his blood pumping. Was Sally here to tell him she carried his child?

As quickly as anticipation rose, it crashed again. No, surely not. It was too soon.

"Sir Charles?" Willis prompted, and he realized he was still staring at the note.

He looked up to meet his butler's impassive gaze. Willis could convey all the animation of a block of wood, when he wanted to. "You haven't left her on the step, have you?"

"No, sir. I showed the lady into the drawing room." He added with purpose, even if his expression didn't change. "Nobody else observed her entrance. I was in the hall when she arrived."

"Good man." Charles suddenly smiled at his butler. "Remind me to raise your salary."

Willis blinked at this sudden change to cheerfulness in a master who had been like a bear with a sore head all week. "Yes, sir. Thank you. Shall I show the lady in here?"

"No, Willis. I'll go to her. You and the rest of the staff may retire for the night. I won't require anything more, and I'll be happy to show my visitor out, once our business is concluded."

He hoped to hell he wasn't lying about being happy. Although given Sally had delivered his marching orders a week ago, he couldn't imagine what she was doing here unless she'd changed her mind about accepting his proposal.

"Yes, Sir Charles." Willis bowed. "Good night."

"Good night, Willis." He paused. "And thank you."

Was that a glint in his butler's gimlet eye? "My pleasure, sir."

What the devil did this unexpected visit mean? Charles's gut churned with an unsettling mixture of expectation and trepidation.

Had Sally come to accept his offer of marriage? Or had she called to say a final goodbye?

No, by God, he wouldn't let that be so. He shouldn't have given up on her—although the woman who left *Sans Souci* had been locked away behind an impenetrable wall of ice, thicker than ever after her lapse of control.

Well, ice could melt, and there was a key for every

lock. Sally had met her match, even if she didn't know it yet.

Once he was alone, Charles sucked in a deep breath as he ran his hands through his hair in an attempt to settle its wild disorder. In the last week, he'd barely picked up a comb, and he was wearing an old shirt, definitely not suitable for receiving company. But be damned if he'd waste time going upstairs to tidy himself up.

With a purpose that had deserted him during these vile days of yearning and despair, he marched out of his library, across the shadowy hall, and into the drawing room.

He paused in the open doorway and took in the tall, slender woman swathed in black veiling. It had only been a week since he'd seen her, but the immediate power of Sally's presence struck him like a blow from a mallet.

His heart crashed against his ribs and every drop of moisture dried from his mouth, so it was an effort to speak. "How the devil you can see an inch in front of your face with all that falderal floating around you is beyond me."

She lifted away the funereal bonnet, and he stepped forward to take it from her and place it on a chair. She was pale and resolute, and her eyes were huge in her thin face. He couldn't read her expression as she stripped off her black kid gloves, but he didn't sense any hostility. "I didn't have to come far."

She didn't sound upset at his unloverlike greeting. He was beyond hedging his questions. "So why did you come?"

"I needed to talk to you."

"Just talk?"

The look she sent him was guarded. "I wasn't sure you'd see me. I've been horrid to you."

So perhaps not just to talk. It was a good sign that she avoided his question.

He curled his hands into fists and fought the urge to seize her and demand she tell him that she was coming back to him. "I'll always welcome you, Sally. Don't you know that yet?"

"So you forgive me for being so cruel?" She linked trembling hands at her waist, and he realized she was nervous.

He shrugged. "It's forgotten."

Charles meant it. With her here, old resentment found no place in his heart.

He read the signs of recent strain in her face. A tightness around her mouth, and blue shadows under her eyes. Was it too much to hope that over these last days, she'd suffered just as he had?

"You're so generous, Charles. When I don't deserve your kindness."

He stepped further into the room and shut the door behind him. Had this lovely, spirited, fragile creature come to entrust herself to him? He prayed it was so. But he remained careful. He'd come so perilously close to losing her once. He didn't want her running away again.

Because if she did, this time it would be forever.

"Did you only come here to ask my forgiveness? You could have done that in a letter."

"I…" She swallowed, and the hands she raised to undo the long line of buttons on her pelisse were shaking so badly, they fumbled. "I heard you were going to Italy."

"I couldn't see any point in staying in England," he said somberly, then with sudden impatience, stepped closer and brushed her hands aside. "Let me do that. You'll be there until Doomsday."

"Yes, Charles," she said, with a docility that he'd never heard from her before.

Quickly and efficiently, he released the buttons and helped her out of her coat. Then he stood back, awe-struck. "Good God, I'm glad Willis didn't see that dress, or he'd have had a heart attack."

Sally glanced down at the bright red silk gown and made an apologetic gesture. "It seemed a gown a scarlet woman would wear."

He paused to admire the sight of her lean, graceful form in the scandalously low-cut dress. The vivid color made her skin look like new cream. It had been diffi-cult enough keeping his hands off her before. Now she stood before him dressed for seduction, it was nigh impossible.

He swallowed and strove to keep his tone light,

when all he wanted was to sweep her into his arms and kiss all the nonsense out of her. "It's certainly scarlet."

"I...I didn't want you mistaking my motives," she muttered, a delightful blush staining her slanted cheekbones.

Shock slammed into him, along with a huge wave of desire. And a renewed surge of hope.

But he'd learned the hard way that they needed to establish some rules before he rushed her into bed. They wanted each other, but passion wasn't their problem, trust was.

He drew himself up to his full height and fought to steady his voice. "Just what are your motives, Sally? A quick tupping, then goodbye, and me off for Italy in the morning? Or something...else?"

"Is something else still an option?" Her expression was searching, and she bit her lip. "Or has my behavior proven that you're better off making for the hills and never seeing me again?"

He inhaled to feed his aching lungs. The damnable thing was he kept forgetting to breathe. "I told you—there's no blame."

"There should be." She went back to twisting her hands together. "I hurt you."

What was the point of lying? Without looking, he dropped her pelisse over a chair. "Yes."

With a remorseful gesture, she spread her hands. "I can't bear that."

He frowned. "So you're here as a way of apologizing?"

"Yes. No." She sucked in an audible breath. "Oh, Charles, will you really make me say it?"

"It depends what you have to say, doesn't it?" He folded his arms and regarded her with unwavering attention. "We've had too many misunderstandings already. It's time to be frank. What do you want from me, Sally?"

Her shuddering breath threatened to send her bosom overflowing from that daring dress. Then she stiffened her spine, and the nervously twisting hands dropped to her sides.

"You. I want you."

Another jolt of desire. The words sizzled through him like flame. But he remained chary about seeing only what he wanted to see. He'd done that at *Sans Souci* and paid an agonizing price.

"Tonight? Or forever?"

She licked her lips, and he fought the urge to grab her and kiss her and have her, whatever her intentions in coming to him tonight. The quiet house around them did nothing to shore up gentlemanly impulses.

"Tonight." She paused as devastation made his heart slam to a stop. Then she went on in a faint voice. "And forever. If you'll have me."

It took him a moment to realize what she'd said. He'd braced for an answer that dashed his dreams all over again.

Still, he didn't move, although the need to touch her was a fever in his blood. "You'd better mean that, Sally. I'm not going through this again."

To his surprise, amusement lit her green eyes. "Good God, Charles, this is like negotiating a legal contract."

He smiled back as certainty, solid as a mountain, settled deep and eternal inside him. "You are, my love. The sort of contract that lasts till death do us part."

She frowned faintly. "So you still mean marriage?"

"I do," he said, echoing the vows he soon hoped to speak in front of a vicar. "Do you?"

She raised her chin and regarded him directly. "I do." Her slender throat worked as she swallowed again. "Now, for pity's sake, Charles, kiss me."

A bolt of happiness struck him, made his head reel. "My darling," he whispered reverently. "You make me the happiest man in England."

With unsteady hands, he caught her by the waist and dragged her up for a hungry kiss. She sighed in satisfaction and wrapped her arms around him with unconcealed possessiveness.

It felt like an eon since he'd touched her. The heat flaring between them was even more incandescent than he remembered. And in seven sleepless nights, by God, he'd done a lot of remembering.

Her familiar scent, smoky rose, flooded his head. Her salty taste fed his rapacious senses. As if she, too, had starved for this connection, her eager tongue swept into his mouth.

His heart pounding, he edged her back until she met the wall behind her. Greedy hands wrenched her bodice down. They both groaned their pleasure when he cupped her breasts.

Breathlessly, she pulled far away enough to see his face. Joy transfigured her. He'd never seen her look so beautiful, nor so open. At last, she'd stepped beyond that wall of glass that had kept her safe from hurt.

She hadn't yet spoken her love, but as he met her glowing eyes, he saw what she felt. Poignant emotion mixed with rising desire.

Damn him for a lucky dog. She was a woman in a million.

"Sir Charles, what on earth are you doing?" The mocking smile curling her lips only made his blood beat harder.

He dragged his hands through her hair, sending a hail of pins scattering over the carpet. Dark gold silk tumbled down around her unforgettable face, turning her into a wild creature. "My dear Lady Norwood, I believe the technical term is pouncing."

Sally had time for a gasp of laughter, then Charles was kissing her again, with more of that tumultuous passion that she craved. A throbbing, now familiar weight set up in the base of her belly, and she shifted to ease the hungry itch between her legs. He was hard and ready, and excitement fizzed through her as she reached down to shape her hand around the impressive bulge in his trousers.

"Oh, yes," he hissed, leaning into her in encouragement.

He pulled away far enough to haul his shirt over his head. She gave a soft growl of appreciation and ran her hands over his chest. The rasp of crisp dark hair beneath her palms was one more glorious sensation.

He kissed her again. She shivered with anticipation when she felt the slow upward slide of her silk skirts.

His hands reached her thighs, and he paused. Then he released a soft exclamation of surprise against her lips. "By heaven, I love you."

A breathless giggle emerged. "Now you know I arrived with wicked intentions."

"Do your worst," he said, stroking along her bare legs and making her shiver.

Deciding not to wear drawers tonight had seemed like boneheaded optimism when she'd left her house. She hadn't even been sure Charles would see her, let alone want to touch her. Now the glitter in his eyes made her glad she'd chosen such a brazen course.

His seeking fingers found her cleft, and she shuddered as he explored her with sensual purpose. She trembled when he slid one long finger into her, then two. As liquid female pleasure greeted his incursions, she tugged his trousers open and closed her hand around rampant flesh.

He groaned and bent his head to her neck, scraping his teeth across her skin until she cried out and tightened her grip on him. The combination of the sting with the rhythmic thrust of his fingers sent her toppling over into a climax that left her knees like water.

"Charles…" she breathed, clinging to him and tracing a line of kisses across his collarbone. "Oh, Charles."

"I love it when you say my name," he gritted out. "I thought you'd call me Sir Charles until the day I died."

"Sir Charles was too much of a gentleman to do this."

"Don't you believe it, darling," he said. "Lift your leg and hook it behind my hips."

"Yes, Charles."

A soft huff of laughter escaped him. "You've become very biddable lately."

She gave a choked giggle as she curled her leg around him, allowing him wanton access. "If you keep me feeling like this, I suspect I'll always be biddable."

"Now there's a delightful challenge," he murmured.

He caught her under her buttocks and lifted her into his body. She strained toward him as need blazed through her, incinerating everything but love.

She gasped as he pushed forward, and her grip on

his shoulders tightened. The pressure between her legs turned into a rapturous fullness.

Once they were fully joined, he went still and lifted his head to stare down into her face. His eyes blazed brilliant in his face, and he looked breathtakingly fierce. "Say you're mine."

She met that uncompromising gaze and read an unconditional love she'd never until this moment believed existed. "I'm yours."

"Always remember that." He drew out so slowly that she saw stars. Then he slid forward with a ruthlessness that left her gasping. The torrent of thrills rippling through her began to build into a tidal wave.

She closed her eyes and joined Charles on the journey to bliss. Just before the sensations inside her exploded into dazzling release, she opened her eyes. "I love you, Charles."

"Sally…" he said on a long groan and thrust into her hard, sending her soaring into a realm of fire.

As the tremors subsided and she drifted down from the stellar heights, she felt wrung out, complete, sated.

Loved.

Poignant gratitude welled inside her, made speech impossible. To think, she'd nearly let her fears deny her this ecstasy, this unearthly closeness.

Well, she was no longer frightened. She was brave and forthright, and confident that she'd found the man she wanted to spend the rest of her life with.

She hid her flushed face in his bare shoulder and

kissed his skin, the tang of his clean sweat sharp in her nostrils. And she spoke again the words she'd never said to anyone until tonight. She was surprised how easily they emerged.

"I love you, Charles."

"And I love you," he said. When his arms closed around her, she knew she'd reached safe harbor at last.

Charles carried a sleepy Sally across to a large armchair beside the unlit hearth. Her declaration of love still echoed in his ears. The whole world glowed, now he knew that she loved him. He'd waited so long to hear those words, he couldn't yet take them for granted. If fate allowed him the privilege, he hoped to hear her say she loved him every day for the rest of their long life together.

Happy beyond his dearest hopes, gloriously satisfied, he settled in the chair and arranged her in his lap. She looked thoroughly ravished. Her bodice sagged over her lovely breasts, offering him a glimpse of sweet strawberry nipples. Her gilt hair cascaded about her. Her lips were red and swollen after his kisses, and her pale skin showed pink where his whiskers had chafed her.

"That was lovely," she murmured, resting her ruffled head on his bare shoulder.

"It was. Although I promise next time we'll be in a

bed." He paused. "And I'll take the time to undress you. In fact, I'll just take my time."

She gave a soft laugh and nestled closer. "That will be nice."

"I'll get a special license today. I don't want next time to be too far away." Nor did he place too much reliance on her claims to barrenness. He wanted no sidelong looks if she bore a child nine months from now. And after the last, difficult days, he intended to claim her as quickly and as permanently as he could.

"I don't either." When she sighed, her breath was warm on his chest. "I wish I could stay tonight."

His hold tightened. "I do, too, but you have to set an example to Meg."

"I know." She met his eyes. "If we're getting married in a few days, I suppose I'll have to let her stay in London after all."

His lips twitched. "And forgive her for interfering."

"She's a minx."

"Undoubtedly."

She gave a gurgle of laughter. "Oh, my goodness, everyone is going to be so surprised when they find out we're getting married."

Charles hid a secret smile. He had a suspicion the only person surprised at this particular outcome was Sally herself. Most of their friends knew where his interest tended.

Sally sat up and kissed him with leisurely enjoyment. "We have so much to do," she said. "And you have to cancel your trip to Italy."

He felt so elated, he was ready to take wing and fly to Venice. As long as she flew with him. "Not necessarily."

"Charles?"

"We could go there for our honeymoon. It only means delaying my journey a week or so."

Her eyes turned brilliant green. "Italy? *Oh, Charles.*"

He smiled down at her, pleased with her reaction to his suggestion. "I'd much rather have you for company than a broken heart."

The light in her eyes faded, and she placed her hand on the side of his face in a gesture of apology. "Oh, my dear, I've hurt you so badly, and all because I was too stupid to know what I wanted."

"What changed your mind? You sounded so certain that you wanted nothing to do with me when we left *Sans Souci.*"

When he saw the shadows come back into her eyes, he was sorry he asked. "I was such a fool. I should have believed you when you told me you loved me."

"Didn't you?"

"Yes, I did." Remorse turned her voluptuous lips downward. "I just didn't trust that your love would last."

"But now you do." It wasn't a question.

When she smiled at him with a return of rapturous happiness, his heart crashed hard against his ribs. He realized that she'd at last left past sorrows behind and looked forward to their glorious future.

So did he, by God. She was everything he wanted. What a life they were going to have together.

"Now I do. I've been so unhappy all week—then Morwenna reminded me that real love is worth every risk."

"God bless Morwenna," he said fervently.

"Yes," Sally murmured. "She gave me the courage to come to you. I'm sorry I was frightened for so long."

He brought her head down for another kiss. "You can spend the next fifty years making it up to me."

She smiled against his lips. "I promise I will." Then in a low, urgent voice, she said, "I love you so very much."

He drew away, cradling her face between his palms and studying those fascinating features that had caught his heart from the first. "I swear I'll make you happy, my love."

Her wanton glance whipped his blood into a hot storm of desire. "There's no time like the present to launch such an admirable project."

Supreme happiness rang in his laugh. "Then, my darling, you and I are in complete agreement."

ABOUT THE AUTHOR

ANNA CAMPBELL has written 10 multi award-winning historical romances for Grand Central Publishing and Avon HarperCollins, and her work is published in 22 languages. She has also written 21 bestselling independently published romances, including her series, The Dashing Widows and The Lairds Most Likely. Anna has won numerous awards for her Regency-set stories including Romantic Times Reviewers Choice, the Booksellers Best, the Golden Quill (three times), the Heart of Excellence (twice), the Write Touch, the Aspen Gold (twice) and the Australian Romance Readers Association's favorite historical romance (five times). Her books have three times been nominated for Romance Writers of America's prestigious RITA Award, and three times for Australia's Romantic Book of the Year. When she's not traveling the world seeking inspiration for her stories, Anna lives on the beautiful east coast of Australia.

Anna loves to hear from her readers. You can find her at:

Website: www.annacampbell.com

facebook.com/AnnaCampbellFans

twitter.com/AnnaCampbellOz

bookbub.com/authors/anna-campbell

goodreads.com/AnnaCampbell

ALSO BY ANNA CAMPBELL

Claiming the Courtesan

Untouched

Tempt the Devil

Captive of Sin

My Reckless Surrender

Midnight's Wild Passion

The Sons of Sin series:

Seven Nights in a Rogue's Bed

Days of Rakes and Roses

A Rake's Midnight Kiss

What a Duke Dares

A Scoundrel by Moonlight

Three Proposals and a Scandal

The Dashing Widows:

The Seduction of Lord Stone

Tempting Mr. Townsend

Winning Lord West

Pursuing Lord Pascal

Charming Sir Charles

Catching Captain Nash

Lord Garson's Bride

The Lairds Most Likely:

The Laird's Willful Lass

The Laird's Christmas Kiss

The Highlander's Lost Lady

Christmas Stories:

The Winter Wife

Her Christmas Earl

A Pirate for Christmas

Mistletoe and the Major

A Match Made in Mistletoe

The Christmas Stranger

Other Books:

These Haunted Hearts

Stranded with the Scottish Earl

THE SEDUCTION OF LORD STONE

(The Dashing Widows Book 1)

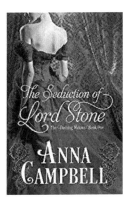

For this reckless widow, love is the most dangerous game of all.

Caroline, Lady Beaumont, arrives in London seeking excitement after ten dreary years of marriage and an even drearier year of mourning. That means conquering society, dancing like there's no tomorrow, and taking a lover to provide passion without promises. Promises, in this dashing widow's dictionary, equal prison. So what is an adventurous lady to do when she loses her heart to a notorious rake who, for the first time in his life, wants forever?

Devilish Silas Nash, Viscount Stone is in love at last with a beautiful, headstrong widow bent on playing the field. Worse, she's enlisted his help to set her up with his disreputable best friend. No red-blooded man takes such a challenge lying down, and Silas schemes to seduce his darling into his arms, warm, willing and besotted. But will his passionate plots come undone against a woman determined to act the mistress, but never the wife?

TEMPTING MR TOWNSEND

(The Dashing Widows Book 2)

Beauty...

Fenella, Lady Deerham has rejoined society after five years
of mourning her beloved husband's death at Waterloo. Now
she's fêted as a diamond of the first water and London's
perfect lady. But beneath her exquisite exterior, this delicate
blond beauty conceals depths of courage and passion nobody
has ever suspected. When her son and his school friend go
missing, she vows to find them whatever it takes. Including
setting off alone in the middle of the night with high-handed
bear of a man, Anthony Townsend.

Will this tumultuous journey end in more tragedy? Or will
the impetuous quest astonish this Dashing Widow with a
breathtaking new love, and life with the last man she ever
imagined?

And the Beast?

When Anthony Townsend bursts into Lady Deerham's fashionable Mayfair mansion demanding the return of his orphaned nephew, the lovely widow's beauty and spirit turn his world upside down. But surely such a refined and aristocratic creature will scorn a rough, self-made man's courtship, even if that man is now one of the richest magnates in England. Especially after he's made such a woeful first impression by barging into her house and accusing her of conniving with the runaways. But when Fenella insists on sharing the desperate search for the boys, fate offers Anthony a chance to play the hero and change her mind about him.

Will reluctant proximity convince Fenella that perhaps Mr. Townsend isn't so beastly after all? Or now that their charges are safe, will Anthony and Fenella remain forever opposites fighting their attraction?

WINNING LORD WEST

(The Dashing Widows Book 3)

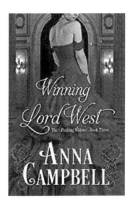

All rakes are the same! Except when they're not...

Spirited Helena, Countess of Crewe, knows all about profligate rakes; she was married to one for nine years and still bears the scars. Now this Dashing Widow plans a life of glorious freedom where she does just what she wishes – and nobody will ever hurt her again.

So what is she to do when that handsome scoundrel Lord West sets out to make her his wife? Say no, of course. Which is fine, until West focuses all his sensual skills on changing her mind. And West's sensual skills are renowned far and wide as utterly irresistible…

Passionate persuasion!

Vernon Grange, Lord West, has long been estranged from his headstrong first love, Helena Nash, but he's always regretted that he didn't step in to prevent her disastrous marriage.

Now Helena is free, and this time, come hell or high water, West won't let her escape him again.

His weapon of choice is seduction, and in this particular game, he's an acknowledged master. Now that he and Helena are under one roof at the year's most glamorous house party, he intends to counter her every argument with breathtaking pleasure. Could it be that Lady Crewe's dashing days are numbered?

PURSUING LORD PASCAL

(The Dashing Widows Book 4)

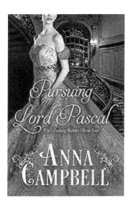

Golden Days...

Famous for her agricultural innovations, Amy, Lady
Mowbray has never had a romantical thought in her life.
Well, apart from her short-lived crush on London's
handsomest man, Lord Pascal, when she was a brainless 14-
year-old. She even chose her late husband because he owned
the best herd of beef cattle in England!

But fate steps in and waltzes this practical widow out of her
rustic retreat into the glamour of the London season. When
Pascal pursues her, all her adolescent fantasies come true.
Those fantasies turn disturbingly adult when grown-up
desire enters the equation. Amy plunges headlong into a
reckless affair that promises pleasure beyond her wildest
dreams – until she discovers that this glittering world hides
damaging secrets and painful revelations set to break a
country girl's tender heart.

All that glitters...

Gervaise Dacre, Lord Pascal needs to marry money to save his estate, devastated after a violent storm. He's never much liked his reputation as London's handsomest man, but it certainly comes in handy when the time arrives to seek a rich bride. Unfortunately, the current crop of debutantes bores him silly, and he finds himself praying for a sensible woman with a generous dowry.

When he meets Dashing Widow Amy Mowbray, it seems all his prayers have been answered. Until he finds himself in thrall to the lovely widow, and his mercenary quest becomes dangerously complicated. Soon he's much more interested in passion than in pounds, shillings and pence. What happens if Amy discovers the sordid truth behind his whirlwind courtship? And if she does, will she see beyond his original, selfish motives to the ardent love that lies unspoken in his sinful heart?

CATCHING CAPTAIN NASH

(The Dashing Widows Book 6)

Home is the sailor, home from the sea...

Five years after he's lost off the coast of South America, presumed dead, Captain Robert Nash escapes cruel captivity, and returns to London and the bride he loves, but barely knows. When he stumbles back into the family home, he's appalled to find himself gate-crashing the party celebrating his wife's engagement to another man.

This gallant naval officer is ready to take on any challenge; but five years is a long time, and beautiful, passionate Morwenna has clearly found a life without him. Can he win back the wife who gave him a reason to survive his ordeal? Or will the woman who haunts his every thought remain eternally out of reach?

Love lost and found? Or love lost forever?

Since hearing of her beloved husband's death, Morwenna

Nash has been mired in grief. After five bleak years without him, she must summon every ounce of courage and determination to become a Dashing Widow and rejoin the social whirl. She owes it to her young daughter to break free of old sorrow and find a new purpose in life, even if that means accepting a loveless marriage.

It's a miracle when Robert returns from the grave, and despite the awkward circumstances of his arrival, she's overjoyed that her husband has come back to her at last. But after years of suffering, he's not the handsome, laughing charmer she remembers. Instead he's a grim shadow of his former dashing self. He can't hide how much he still wants her—but does passion equal love?

Can Morwenna and Robert bridge the chasm of absence, suffering and mistrust, and find their way back to each other?

LORD GARSON'S BRIDE

(The Dashing Widows Book 7)

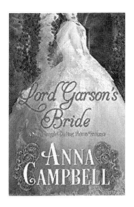

Lord Garson's dilemma.

Hugh Rutherford, Lord Garson, loved and lost when his
fiancée returned to the husband she'd believed drowned. In
the three years since, Garson has come to loathe his
notoriety as London's most famous rejected suitor. It's high
time to find a bride, a level-headed, well-bred lady who will
accept a loveless marriage and cause no trouble. Luckily he
has just the candidate in mind.

A marriage of convenience...

When Lady Jane Norris receives an unexpected proposal
from her childhood friend Lord Garson, marriage to the
handsome baron rescues her from a grim future. At twenty-
eight, Jane is on the shelf and under no illusions about her
attractions. With her father's death, she's lost her home and
faces life as an impecunious spinster. While she's aware

Garson will never love again, they have friendship and goodwill to build upon. What can possibly go wrong?

...becomes very inconvenient indeed.

From the first, things don't go to plan, not least because Garson soon finds himself in thrall to his surprisingly intriguing bride. A union grounded in duty veers toward obsession. And when the Dashing Widows take Jane in hand and transform her into the toast of London, Garson isn't the only man to notice his wife's beauty and charm. He's known Jane all her life, but suddenly she's a dazzling stranger. This isn't the uncomplicated, pragmatic match he signed up for. When Jane defies the final taboo and asks for his love, her impossible demand threatens to blast this convenient marriage to oblivion.

Once the dust settles, will Lord Garson still be the man who can only love once?

Manufactured by Amazon.ca
Bolton, ON